"You were upset because you still love me."

"No!" Leah knew she was talking rubbish, and so did Hogan. "The physical side of our love affair...was good. But we function better on a platonic level."

"Better?" The water eddied around them as he pressed closer, gliding against her. "Feel what you do to me! There's nothing platonic about that." His hand drifted to cradle her breast, caressing the peak with his thumb. "And there's nothing platonic about that, either!"

His fingers moved to catch her chin, tilting it until she was forced to accept his need and reveal her answering desire.

"We've tried it both ways, kitten. Now we'll try the third and final way. Tonight we'll sleep together," he murmured. "And every night...."

"Until you leave Hong Kong!" she blurted out.

Books by Elizabeth Oldfield

These books may be available at your local bookseller.

Don't miss any of our special offers. Write to us at the
following address for information on our newest releases.

Harlequin Reader Service
P.O. Box 52040, Phoenix, AZ 85072-2040
Canadian address: P.O. Box 2800, Postal Station A,
5170 Yonge St., Willowdale, Ont. M2N 5T5

ELIZABETH OLDFIELD

too far, too fast

Harlequin Books

TORONTO • NEW YORK • LONDON
AMSTERDAM • PARIS • SYDNEY • HAMBURG
STOCKHOLM • ATHENS • TOKYO • MILAN

Harlequin Presents first edition January 1985
ISBN 0-373-10758-7

Original hardcover edition published in 1984
by Mills & Boon Limited

CHAPTER ONE

A HIGH-PITCHED crackle screamed along the international telephone wire and Leah winced.

'Hogan's a red-hot commodity,' Saul was bellowing. There came a second crackle, a second wince. 'He's big business, honey, and I mean *big*.'

Leah sighed, massaging the tingle from her ear. It was sheer bedlam, her boss's phone calls usually were. When he was enthusiastic, which was ninety-nine point nine per cent of the time, he yelled. He was yelling now and despite the eight thousand miles of land and sea which separated the New York head office from Leah in Hong Kong, his bull-roar came over several decibels too loud. Without warning the crackling faded, doubtless acknowledging defeat by a superior force, and Leah heard herself speaking into silence.

'I'm well aware of how successful Hogan is at merchandising his assets!' she retorted.

Sensitivity was not Saul's strong point so the comment was taken at face value.

'Adding the glamour boy dimension was a shrewd move on our part,' he said, with a self-congratulatory chuckle. 'The women drool over him.'

'You didn't have to "add" much.' Leah was unable to keep the scorn from her voice. 'He's always been lean, dark and moody-looking, and from what I hear his love-life provides endless copy for the media.'

Deaf to her sarcasm, Saul boomed delighted approval: 'We're handling him just right. He's one hell of a money-earner and it's all thanks to the expertise of Spencer Associates,' he continued, determined to claim credit, come what may.

'No thanks to me,' muttered Leah, poking a disobedient strand of shiny flaxen hair back into her topknot. As head of the South-East Asian branch of Saul Spencer Associates, a leading public relations firm, she was far removed from Hogan Whitney's sphere of activity in Europe and the States, a circumstance which suited her to perfection. Unfortunately fate, in the unstoppable form of Saul Spencer, publicist *extraordinaire*, had now decreed Hogan was to visit Hong Kong. She frowned, leaning forward to riffle through the papers on her desk. 'He appears to have a remarkable list of commercial sponsors, everything from sports watches to racing cars.'

'Claws in half a million dollars annually from endorsements alone,' confirmed Saul. 'He used to dominate tennis, but now he's dominating the get-rich-quick scene. And don't forget we take a hefty percentage of all he earns!' She could almost hear him rubbing his hands together in mercenary glee. Money was Saul's god, his reason for living, and now it seemed Hogan was worshipping at the same altar. 'He'll only be with you for a week so squeeze in as many personal appearances as you can,' her boss continued. 'Hogan has an easy-going manner with the public. He'll have them eating out of his hand in Hong Kong.'

Leah made a face at the telephone. 'Don't worry, I've already set the ball rolling.'

'Fix television interviews and brief the newspapers.' Saul stampeded on regardless. 'He handles himself well with the press. There's his book on tennis for beginners to promote, and a video——'

'Okay, okay.' She dammed the flow of instructions midstream, not wishing to hear more; the details were in the file anyway.

Saul's forte was organisation and though his company now functioned on a worldwide basis he perpetually itched to be involved at grass roots. Leah knew from experience that given half a chance he would be running the whole show himself. Uneasily she fingered the jabot frill at the neck of her lilac taffeta blouse. Of late she had become increasingly aware that Saul Spencer's ways were not her ways. He was a bold, brash character who revelled in the showbiz aspect of public relations. Give him a 'personality' and he became a regular Phineas Barnum, promoting with a shameless exaggeration which made her cringe. In truth she preferred not to deal with individuals—publicising products or company images was far more satisfying, and safer . . .

'Sorry, honey, I guess I'm poking my nose in unnecessarily.' He gave an ear-splitting burst of laughter which made her wince a third time. 'How's the deal working out with that Tan guy?'

'Great!' Leah could relax now, she was back on firm ground. 'The first collection of casual wear brought in enquiries from far and wide, and several good orders resulted. I'm seeing Mr Tan this morning to discuss a trade exhibition which is scheduled for the spring. A stand would give excellent exposure, all the big names will be showing.' Her smooth brow creased. 'Unfortunately he's so pleased with the way we've promoted his products that now he's trying to lumber us with his daughter. Jasmine's a nightclub singer,' she explained. 'Her father thinks she's wonderful, but I have my doubts.' Leah raised her wide green eyes to the ceiling in comic despair. 'She sings in Cantonese and off-key!'

Saul guffawed. 'Humour him. Mr Tan's worth a fortune to us, so keep him sweet.'

'Jasmine's not in our line at all,' she grumbled, tapping rose-lacquered nails on the desk top in irritation. 'I've tried to make Mr Tan understand that, but he insists we can help her career. I'm wondering how I can wriggle out of handling her affairs without causing both her and her father to lose face.'

'String them along,' Saul said magnanimously. 'You can afford to carry the odd sprat, so long as we catch the mackerels.' He switched subjects again. 'You're doing a fine job out there, Leah. I was speaking with the chairman of the Dynasty group and he's over the moon about your promotion of the Hong Kong hotel. Congratulations!'

At this morale-booster she beamed, turning sideways to gaze out of the window. Beyond the mile-wide stretch of Victoria Harbour was the mainland, and amongst the clutter of skyscrapers on Kowloon she could pick out the twin towers of the Dynasty Hotel, glimmering white in the winter sunshine. Automatically Leah touched the jade stud in her ear, her mind drifting to Glenn, the Australian manager of the de-luxe hotel. She had an uneasy suspicion that the studs and matching ring, his gift to her at Christmas a few weeks ago, had been expensive, too expensive. And what followed jade—diamonds? Sitting bolt upright she abandoned thoughts of Glenn and snapped her attention back to Saul, answering his fusillade of questions about projects currently on hand.

'Hogan's bitten by the comeback bug, thank God,' he said at length, coming full circle. 'He's level-headed enough to realise an active sports figure is far more promotable than an ex-champ.'

'Didn't you say he was hot?' she asked suspiciously.

'Sure is, but his appeal will cool if he doesn't get back on to the circuit pretty damn quick. He's had eighteen months away from professional tennis as it is and his sponsors only stick in because there's the prospect of him hitting the big time again. Everyone's dying to know if he can resume his former glory and win Wimbledon this time around. If there wasn't the tantalising dilemma of "can he, can't he?" the companies would desert him like rats leaving a sinking ship.' Leah's lip curled. She suspected the first rat to desert Hogan should his fortunes tumble could well be Saul. 'He starts back on the Grand Prix merry-go-round in the spring,' her boss told her. 'And the sooner, the better. His sponsors are pressing for some action.'

'But suppose he doesn't come up trumps?'

'All I ask is that he squeezes back into the top twenty computer ratings and from present form he's perfectly capable of that. Whether he wins or loses the top accolades is no big deal as far as Spencer Associates is concerned. It doesn't bother me,' he added callously.

'It'll bother Hogan!' she retorted.

'Honey, by then he'll have brought us in a fantastic return on our investment. Let's not be greedy.'

Leah shook her head, suspended between incredulity and disgust at Saul's ability to bend any situation to suit his own criteria.

'He's still coasting on the publicity after his accident,' her boss continued. 'That smash-up was the best thing that ever happened to him.'

A wry brow lifted at the assessment. Whether Hogan would agree his car crash eighteen months ago, resulting in serious leg injuries, was the best thing that had ever happened to him, she very much doubted!

'I'm amazed his leg is strong enough for professional tennis,' she said. 'Isn't it held together by steel pins?'

'Sure is. He's bionic like what's-his-name.' There were hoots of laughter. Saul loved jokes, especially his own. 'But you know Hogan, he can't function without a challenge. Total physical commitment, that's the name of his game. He's had a gruelling round of exhibition matches over the winter but the leg's been no problem, honey, no problem.'

Leah frowned at the blithe assurance. Considering a section of his thigh had been rebuilt in complicated surgery, Hogan sounded to have made a dramatic recovery.

When her boss rang off she sat nibbling at a thumbnail. It was galling to realise that for the past eighteen months she had been deluding herself. She had assumed distance and time had provided complete immunity to Hogan's particular brand of charm, but how wrong she had been! The downward dive of her heart at the first glimpse of his dark head on the posters accompanying the information file was warning enough. The psychological barrier she had erected was not as sturdy as she had imagined. Now it seemed little had been changed by her flight to Hong Kong. Indeed, it was possible her feelings had been kept on ice, and no more . . .

Petulantly she pushed aside the bulky folder. Hogan's visit was scheduled for mid-March, two months away, yet already there had been a trickle of enquiries as to when he would arrive. She had been forced to field off invitations from hostesses who knew their star would sparkle more brightly if they achieved the social coup of having the famous Hogan Whitney to dine. Doubtless from the moment his plane touched down at Kai Tak Airport, Hong Kong would be agog, or at least the expatriate population would be. Many of the locals would neither know nor care that a top tennis pro had arrived in their midst, but Leah was aware of a growing band of Western-orientated Chinese who were tennis *aficionados*. They would flock to his personal appearances, buy his books in droves, soak up his advice on backhands and dropshots, and pay hefty sums to marvel at the deadly accuracy with which those backhands and dropshots were demonstrated during his exhibition matches.

Leah flipped open the folder, staring back defiantly into Hogan's cool grey eyes. *Watch a Champion in Action* the blurb ran. Her full lips tightened. She had no wish to be trampled to the ground in that particular rush!

There was a scuffling in the outer office and her door was pushed open in fits and starts before Violet, her secretary, appeared, staggering across the room beneath a wobbly stack of books. Leah glared suspiciously at the top cover where an athletic figure was poised to smash an unsuspecting ball into outer space.

'What are those?' she demanded.

The Chinese girl slid her cargo on to the desk, steadying the pile with tiny fluttering hands. 'Books by Hogan Whitney. A carton has arrived, air-freighted from New York, and there are plenty books, video films, life-size cardboard cut-outs, big coloured photos, tee-shirts——'

'Store everything outside in the cupboard and I'll check it through later.' Leah knew she was avoiding the issue, but right now the prospect of being surrounded by images of Hogan would ruin any chance she had of maintaining her sang-froid.

'Shall I try one of these?' Violet asked eagerly, magpie eyes scrutinising a cellophane-packaged shirt. Violet enjoyed nothing better than a diversion, any excuse to stop typing.

'No!' Belatedly Leah remembered to add, 'Thank you.' She was damned if she wanted to see Hogan's heavy-lidded good looks emblazoned across her secretary's chest.

Violet screwed her face into an attitude of intense concentration. 'Roger said you and Mr Whitney used to be friends. Does he really have go-to-bed eyes?' she giggled.

For once Leah was not amused by the girl's lopsided English. 'It's *come*-to-bed,' she snapped, furious to discover that Roger, her second-in-command, had been indiscreet enough to tell her secretary that she and Hogan knew each other from the past. Violet was a one-girl communications satellite, beaming out the affairs of the 'foreign devils' to a goodly proportion of Hong Kong, or so it seemed. Certainly she kept the multi-storeyed office block humming with gossip. Whenever a snippet of news surfaced Violet would pick up the phone and spread the word, informing Pauline, a receptionist far below in the lobby, and a variety of other contacts. Leah frowned, wondering what else Roger had let slip. He was presently away on leave, but the moment he returned she would make it plain she did not relish having her private life discussed.

Stalking to the space-age coatstand, she ignored Violet's black twinkle of expectancy. Go-to-bed or come-to-bed, it didn't matter much, she thought corrosively shrugging into the jacket of her grey flannel suit. Only meagre whispers of gossip percolated to Hong Kong, but there had been sufficient to indicate Hogan was still as active between the sheets as he was on the tennis courts, if not more so these days. Dedicated to a come-back he might be, and Leah knew the iron discipline he had at his disposal, but no matter how rigorous his fitness regime it was doubtful that women would be eliminated. Hogan was highly-sexed. Who knew the bliss and agony of that better than she! He desired women—*plural*, she told herself brutally, and women desired Hogan.

'All week drizzle, yet today it's like springtime on the Mediterranean,' she said, walking to the vast window behind her desk.

Violet's face fell at the mundane observation. 'But very cold,' she complained, realising there would be no titbits.

Although she was muffled up to the eyebrows in thick-knit sweater and cardigan, the Chinese girl shivered, joining her employer to look out at the January sunshine. The view was spectacular. Spencer Associates occupied a prestigious fifteenth floor suite of offices on the southern shores of Hong Kong Island. Leah's office, identical to all the other branch offices, was sleek and futuristic, lit with dramatic lighting pods. Swedish-designed desk and chairs were fashioned from slats of stainless steel and leather, there was a white velour carpet and on stark walls hung gigantic abstracts in mauve, citrus and wine. The pictures always made her frown. Hogan, with his healthy disrespect for Saul's taste, had sworn gin-crazed gorillas were responsible for the garish daubs. Her boss must have received a good discount for he appeared to have purchased a lorry-

load and similar monstrosities decorated Spencer
Associate offices throughout the world.

Despite the office stating its identity as one of several,
the view was unique. Hong Kong was one of the few
places on earth where man had successfully joined the
forces of nature to create a devastating impact on the
eye. Across the blue straits, where seabirds wheeled
over chugging junks and sampans, was the serrated
skyline of Kowloon; here bustling thoroughfares were
jam-packed with shops, street markets, swarming Asian
life. If you battled free eventually you reached the New
Territories where hills rose green and peaceful and
beyond the New Territories was China, mysterious alien
China.

Leah's working hours were spent either on Hong
Kong Island or in Kowloon, the heart of the Colony
where life was electric. She had never changed her
first impression that Hong Kong was a land of
spun-sugar dreams where nothing was permanent,
where anything was possible. Peasants dreamed of
becoming millionaires, while millionaires dreamed of
becoming billionaires and titled ones, at that. Fortunes
were made and lost overnight in money like Monopoly
money. Giants of glass, steel and concrete were
erected in weeks and demolished with equal speed to
make room for another, more splendid, monolith.
Visitors flew in and out. Share prices rose and fell.
There was always a crisis. Even the weather veered
from one extreme to the other, from terrifying
typhoons to idyllic days when the air was warm and
gentle. Leah smiled at the sunshine glinting on the
water.

'No topcoat?' her secretary exclaimed in horror when
she collected up her clutch purse and gloves. Violet

rubbed at her upper arms swaddled in thick-knit. 'Very cold.'

'You haven't got a clue what cold really means,' Leah teased. 'Heaven knows what would happen if Hong Kong had a fall of snow.' She made for the door. 'Would you telephone Mr Tan, please, and tell him I'm on my way?'

Violet shivered again. 'Will do, Miss Morrison.'

Leah's flaxen hair always brought a reaction, and as she slid on to the wooden bench on the upper deck of the Star Ferry she was aware of the chance glances, fleeting smiles and shrewd calculating stares. Younger men, both Chinese and Caucasian, often tried to catch her eye and sometimes the better-looking ones succeeded, but the older Asians were wary, never quite trusting foreigners, even if they were blonde, slender and pretty. She bit back a smile as she contrasted her light-weight suit with the bulky clothes of the other passengers. Rolypoly Chinese toddlers frolicked, snug in quilted suits of scarlet and royal blue, better equipped for the ski slopes of Switzerland than the sub-tropical shores of the South China Sea.

As the ferry pulled against the quay of the Kowloon terminal the crowds pushed ashore, jostling up the ramp with Leah in their midst. When she found a taxi she arranged herself in the back seat, resigned to a slow journey. Hong Kong traffic reminded her of a cattle round-up with its long pauses, breathless dashes for open space, blaring of horns, shouts, gestures and the crush of too many vehicles buffeting for room in the congested streets.

How would she handle Hogan's visit? Tatters of disquiet persisted and Leah found herself feeling beleaguered once more. She knew she was over-reacting, and if her nerves were in danger of being shot to pieces by the mere sight of his photograph, a mere discussion of his activities, how would she feel when he appeared in the flesh? Folding her arms in rough exasperation, she gave herself a short snappy lecture. She was twenty-five years old, the capable head of a profitable branch of an international public relations company, and here she was, panicking at the prospect of meeting Hogan again. She gave a sour little laugh. A smart cookie she might be in the public relations world, but as far as relations with six-foot-two tennis players were concerned . . .

Her blonde head dipped at an inner decision. The day Hogan flew into Hong Kong would be the day she flew out. It didn't much matter where to, she had business contacts throughout the Far East and could easily drum up meetings in Manila or Tokyo or Bangkok. She would tackle the preliminary work for his visit; organise and advertise the tennis matches, plan his travel arrangements, press conferences and such, but once Roger returned from leave she would hand over complete responsibility to him.

Leah sucked in her lower lip, wrestling with her conscience. Although Roger was only a year younger than she, he could be unnervingly naive. At times he showed very little sense, as his gossiping with Violet had shown. But Hogan would only be in the Colony for a week, so what could go wrong? She scowled out at the pavements where locals and tourists alike crowded around the hawker stalls. Hogan was a perfectionist. He would not react kindly to being off-loaded on to an amateur, and it would not take him long to realise Roger *was* an amateur.

Damn Hogan! Why did he have to march back now, disrupting her life and her thoughts? One thing was certain, he would not be working himself up into a frenzy at the prospect of meeting *her* again after a gap of eighteen months. As far as Hogan was concerned she had been another notch on his gun, a deeper notch than most perhaps, but still only a notch. No, he would be indifferent.

There was a gap in the traffic and the taxi thundered through. Ten minutes later they reached the suburbs where Mr Tan's flatted factory was situated. Determinedly Leah rejected any doubts about the wisdom of allowing Roger to cover Hogan's visit. He would manage, he would *have* to manage! By the time the taxi braked to a halt, her plans were complete.

Mr Tan did not look like a millionaire. He was a small, wiry man in his fifties with greased black hair. Invariably he wore a white nylon shirt, high-necked vest showing through, and baggy grey trousers. He padded around his group of factories in gym shoes, the only hint of wealth being his mouthful of gold teeth. For years his workforce had produced casual wear and designer jeans under other firms' labels, but now his aim was to corner some of this lucrative market for himself. He had telephoned Leah out of the blue the previous summer, asking if Spencer Associates could help and in due course a successful collaboration had evolved.

To complement the well made clothes, she had produced the flair and imagination to successfully market them. Originally the line had been entitled 'Jasmine Modes' after Mr Tan's beloved daughter, but Leah tactfully persuaded him 'Fast-Lane Fashions' would sell better. She had discovered a local girl, trained in Paris, who had designed the first limited collection, and production went ahead. The clothes had been photographed, advertised in magazines and trade papers, press releases and glossy brochures had been issued. Next month would see a television commercial, and plans were afoot to expand the range to Singapore and Malaysia.

After discussing the trade show, Mr Tan sat back in his chair. 'Now we talk about Jasmine,' he said, flashing gold teeth.

Leah groaned inwardly. 'She should get herself on to the books of a theatrical agent, that approach would be best.'

Mr Tan's hands circled in the air like brown moths. 'Poof! agents in Hong Kong lousy. Jasmine would be big star now if agents good. You help, you clever girl. You guide her and make her famous.'

'Jasmine's a pretty girl,' Leah said, playing for time as she wondered how she could ease out of the dilemma in style.

'Very pretty,' her client agreed. 'And good singer.'

'I suppose there's a faint chance I could arrange a spot in the cabaret at the Dynasty Hotel,' she mused, thinking aloud as the idea occurred to her. Surely she could persuade Glenn to agree to a fraction of exposure during some dinnertime performance? Jasmine was a charmer, petite and almond-eyed, and the tourists would never know whether her caterwauling was in tune or not, would they?

Mr Tan grabbed hold of her hand and pumped it up and down, rewarding her with the dazzle of teeth. 'Thank you, thank you. I send my daughter to you when the booking is fixed. You tell her what to wear, what to sing, okay?'

Leah's heart thudded to her boots. Mr Tan's dreams were reflected in his eyes. Now Jasmine was destined to become a world-famous singing star—Barbra Streisand, eat your heart out!

Her problems swirled in her head as she marched determinedly through the crowded streets towards the Dynasty Hotel. First Hogan had cropped up, and now Jasmine. She was skating on thin ice. All it needed was for Roger to break a leg and Glenn to prove uncooperative, and she would be struggling.

'Hi there, beaut,' Glenn said in his flat Australian accent, smiling when she poked her head around his office door. 'Give me a minute.' He rapidly finished a discussion with one of his underlings and sent the youth on his way. His brown eyes were shining as he walked round from his desk, arms open wide, and clasped her to him.

'I'm here on business,' Leah protested, when he aimed a kiss for her mouth. He was a tall, rangy man with wavy brown hair and a friendly exuberance. She allowed him a light kiss on the lips, then pulled back before any further intimacies were taken. 'Business, Glenn,' she repeated.

'What's up?' he asked, reluctantly accepting her formality as she gave his shoulders a little push to disentangle herself. He stood back, hands on hips, smiling at her.

'Do you think you could do me a favour?' The moment the words had been said, Leah felt a pang of remorse. Glenn would never refuse, indeed if she had produced a comb and paper ensemble from Outer Mongolia, he would find space in the cabaret, to please *her*. Leah's green eyes clouded and her opinion of

herself began to plummet; she was using him. Saul
might use people right, left and centre in the name of
success and profit, but that was not her way. 'No,
forget it,' she said, standing up a little straighter.

'Come on, beaut, tell me what it's all about,' he
coaxed.

She gave a sigh of exasperation. 'I was intending to
ask if you could find a few minutes for a Chinese girl
singer in your cabaret, but I'm not playing fair. I heard
her once and she's murder!'

Glenn chuckled. 'All Chinese singers sound dreadful
to me. Have you heard their opera?' He rolled his eyes
in despair then grew thoughtful, walking back to leaf
through some papers on his desk. 'Actually I could
help. We can't take anyone on a permanent basis, but
we're going to be short of singers over the New Year
holiday. The regular girls want time off, so there will be
one or two vacant slots. I could give your protégée a
chance then, would that be okay?' He grinned at Leah's
indecision. 'Frankly there's such chaos at mealtimes at
Chinese New Year that I doubt she'll be heard above
the clatter. Send her along a couple of days before the
festivities and she can have a tune-up with the band.'

'Thanks, just one short spot would be fine. I'm very
grateful. Jasmine does look good, even if she doesn't
sound good,' she said, in an attempt to justify Glenn's
generosity.

'I bet she doesn't look as good as you.' He moved
closer, reaching for her and would have moved closer
still if the telephone had not shrilled into action. He
lifted the receiver, placing a large hand over the
mouthpiece. 'Don't go yet.'

'Glenn, we're both supposed to be working,' Leah
pointed out.

He gave a noisy sigh, admitting the truth of her words. 'Okay, beaut, give me a kiss and off you go.' He grinned, eyes fond, as she did as she was told. 'I'll give you a buzz tonight. I'm involved in split shifts right now, but with luck there'll be a couple of free days at the weekend, we'll get together then,' he promised with a smile.

Leah sent one of her Chinese trainees out to buy pizza and fruit for her lunch, eating distractedly as she waded through the file on Hogan. If anyone had imagined he was all washed-up when his accident terminated a straight run of wins to the quarterfinals at Wimbledon, they were wrong. Her information showed he had picked himself up from his hospital bed and started again to rebuild his career. It could not have been easy, but if anyone could return to top-class tennis at the age of twenty-nine after eighteen months in the wilderness, it was Hogan. He had the aggression, the confidence and the commitment. Winning mattered to him and in the past he had won often. Leah scribbled notes. A suite must be reserved for him at the Dynasty. By using the hotel she was killing two birds with one stone, for Hogan's stay there would bring extra prestige for the chain. Already she had mentioned the prospect of using the all-weather courts in the hotel gardens for the exhibition matches, and Glenn was delighted to co-operate. She made a note to ask about seating arrangements. She was deep in thought when a girlish giggle broke her concentration. Violet was standing in the centre of the room.

'Good, yes?' she asked, opening wide her cardigan to reveal a white tee-shirt.

Hogan's heavy-lidded looks caught Leah unawares.

'Very exciting, but I thought you were cold?' she said in a tight voice.

The stilted response was uncharacteristic and took the Chinese girl by surprise. She giggled, not knowing what to do next and rushed for the door with relief when the telephone rang on the small switchboard in the outer office. Seconds later Leah's intercom buzzed.

She flicked the switch. 'Yes?'

Violet was subdued. 'New York on the line, Miss Morrison.'

'Thanks.' Leah squeezed a little extra warmth into the word. It was not her secretary's fault if she was bogged down with thoughts of Hogan and that the sight of the tee-shirt had sent her spirits nose-diving with a resounding zonk.

'Saul here, honey,' her boss yelled. 'Problems with our tennis star, I'm afraid.'

'He can't come?' She tried not to sound too hopeful.

There was a loud growl of determination. 'He's coming. He'll visit Hong Kong if I deliver him there myself in a strait-jacket.'

'Doesn't he want to come?' Leah was contritely vexed. The idea that Hogan might have reservations about meeting her again flooded her with unreasonable chagrin. How dare he!

'He reckons he deserves a break from the publicity treadmill,' her boss explained. 'Though God knows why.'

She recalled the long list of towns, cities and countries Hogan had visited in recent months. 'Maybe the travelling is getting him down?'

'Nah!' Saul spurned the idea. 'He's been on the move since he was a teenager following the tennis circuit, so a few interviews and exhibition matches aren't going to bother him, are they?'

She recalled their earlier discussion. 'You said yourself they were gruelling.'

'Nothing Hogan can't cope with,' he replied carelessly. As usual Saul was intent on having it both ways. 'He's just raising a little hell. Must have got out of the wrong side of the bed this morning.'

Leah resisted the urge to ask whose bed, for an up-to-date resumé of Hogan's love affairs was the last thing she needed. Her brow furrowed as she scanned the folder. 'He's been on the go non-stop for several months, surely he's exhausted by the constant crowds?'

'Nah!' Saul shattered through her reasoning like a bull in a china shop.

'Maybe he gets tired more easily since his accident. I'm sure his leg must——'

Her boss cut in again. 'He works out in the gym every day, does calisthenics non-stop, rides bikes over mountains. The guy's dedicated.'

'He's still human! Why don't you arrange for him to miss Hong Kong and have a holiday? Surely that would suit him?' It would suit *me*, she added silently.

'Nah, Hong Kong's a money-maker. What I intend is to scrap his New Zealand itinerary, that'll cut out a helluva lot of travelling, and reschedule his visit to you.' There was a pause while Saul calculated under his breath. 'He'll arrive at the beginning of February.' He gave her the dates.

Blood rushed to Leah's head. Roger would still be away over the period Paul specified. 'He can't come then!' she shrieked. 'It's Chinese New Year,' she continued, forcing her voice down to a respectable level. 'Everything stops dead. The locals disappear to visit relations and friends. The expats, well . . . they go off on holiday. The place is deserted.' She was lying through her teeth, mind buzzing. If Hogan arrived in February she would be forced to take charge. Apart from Roger her staff consisted of two young trainees and there was no way she could dump Hogan on them. 'Invariably it's wet at Chinese New Year,' she added, warming to her theme. 'A big grey cloud comes down and it's miserable. His tennis matches will be rained off.'

'Fix them indoors.' Saul brushed aside her remarks as unworthy quibbles. 'He can do the rounds for five or six days and take a second week as a holiday. Hawaii is his destination after Hong Kong, I need him fresh for that.'

Two weeks of Hogan! 'Why can't he have his holiday in Hawaii?' she demanded, and it came out as a wail.

'He's too well-known there, he'd never have a moment's peace. It'll be more relaxed in Hong Kong, he'll be able to get around without being recognised too much,' said Saul reasonably.

'There could be problems fixing up his visit at such short notice.' Leah was hanging on by her fingertips.

'You'll manage. Don't I employ you for your skill in such matters?' Her boss gave a light touch of the whip to remind her who called the tune. 'Incidentally Hogan refuses to stay at a hotel, says he's sick of them. He wants somewhere private.' She went very still, wondering what was coming next. 'I seem to remember Roger will be on leave early February, so Hogan can use his apartment.'

'He won't like it,' she blurted out. 'It's very small, there's hardly room to swing a cat.' The excuse was all she could dredge up on the spur of the moment.

'Hogan is not in the cat-swinging business,' said Saul

in a loud peremptory voice which left little doubt that
his patience was fast running out.

There was no alternative but to close the telephone
call with as much grace as she could muster, and then
Leah sat silent, pressing a fist against her forehead. A
dull weight was forming in her stomach. She was
cornered. In three weeks' time she was destined to play
the gracious hostess, the skivvy, the maid, in fact
whatever role he decreed, to a grey-eyed muscle
machine with a husky drawl and devastating sex-
appeal. She pulled herself up into stiff-backed defiance.
There was one role she was determined she would never
play again—that of Hogan Whitney's lover.

CHAPTER TWO

DURING the three weeks preceding Chinese New Year
Leah's pace, and that of Hong Kong, reached a
feverish canter. By contrast Christmas, a few weeks
past, had been subdued. True the hotels and department
stores had been garlanded with tinsel, and jet-eyed girls
had made adorable 'santarinas' but Leah suspected the
festivities had been a sop to the tourists and expatriates.
Now the Chinese community were celebrating *their*
holiday. Scarlet banners proclaiming *'Kung Hee Fatt
Choy'*—good luck and prosperity, were strung across
the shops, Chinese lanterns appeared in their thousands,
and all manner of sweets and delicacies were on sale at
exorbitant prices. Violet rushed around buying up
mandarin oranges, which were symbols of gold, waxed
ducks, sausages and huge armfuls of pussy-willow.
Crimson charm papers with golden script were fastened
to doorways to ward off evil spirits, homes were
scrubbed clean from top to bottom, and Leah arranged
to give her staff the customary *ang pows*, red packets
containing a thirteenth month's salary.

In one way she was grateful for the distraction of the
forthcoming holiday, for she had little time to resurrect
Hogan as a living, breathing real-life man. Organising
his visit occupied a fair proportion of her working day,
but here she managed to treat him as a 'commodity'.
Arrangements went smoothly. Her media contacts were
delighted by the prospect of having someone as
newsworthy as a topflight ex-champion in town, so

press coverage promised to be heavy. Glenn, as expected, had been immensely supportive, and the exhibition matches would take place on the courts in the hotel grounds, with the proviso that should it rain the venue would be switched indoors.

'We'll shift all the exercising gear from the gymnasium and open up the dividers with the squash courts and basketball arena. Everyone will fit in,' he had assured her. 'Don't worry.'

Glenn's cheerful optimism had bolstered her spirits and if, at Christmas, she had been wary of the way their friendship was developing, now she was grateful. He was a tower of strength and precisely what she needed. Although Leah had exposed only the bare bones of her previous contact with Hogan, the Australian sensed her disquiet and went out of his way to soothe her jumping nerves.

For the umpteenth time Leah checked her list, though she could recite the programme off by heart. Hogan was due to arrive tomorrow afternoon. After a short press conference in the airport's V.I.P. lounge he would be driven to Roger's apartment, just across the corridor from hers, she thought uneasily, and allowed time to recover from his long flight. At seven a limousine had been ordered to take them both to the Dynasty Hotel where they would dine with a lady journalist from one of the Colony's leading magazines. Leah jotted down a reminder that Hogan must be given the opportunity to inspect the tennis courts. She crossed her fingers. He was a stickler for perfection as far as his sport was concerned, and she hoped the courts would meet his high standards. Certainly Glenn had been adamant that the facilities could not be bettered. The exhibition matches had been scheduled for the following day, and the remainder of the week was crammed with book-signings, radio and television interviews, talks and personal appearances. When her intercom buzzed Leah closed the folder.

'Miss Tan to see you,' Violet announced with the customary giggle.

The door burst open and a vivacious cheerleader in white leather shorts, silver bomber jacket and matching thigh-high boots pranced into the room. Leah's green eyes widened in astonishment. She had seen Jasmine only once, when the girl had been performing at a downtown nightclub, and on that occasion she had been the demure Chinese songstress personified. Her midnight-blue cheongsam had been high-necked, her hair combed back into a classical chignon, her complexion chalk-white with bee-stung crimson lips.

'Hi there,' the apparition warbled, jauntily throwing off her jacket to reveal a skimpy silver vest. She plopped herself down in a chair, puffing up her torrent of tight black curls with busy hands. 'How's it going?'

Leah had to struggle to keep her face straight. She had assumed Jasmine would be reticent and shy, not an extrovert whose manner and dress showed more than a passing resemblance to modern Miss America.

'Y.C.'s thrilled at the chance of playing against Hogan Whitney. He reckons he's in with a chance,' the girl smiled, taking a silver cigarette case from her shoulder-bag. 'Smoke?'

'No, thank you.' Leah was busily attempting to gather up her wits.

'Y.C. and I are going steady.'

'Y.C. Wong, you mean?' It was all clicking into place. Y.C. Wong was the Colony's leading tennis player. He was an amateur, but he was good. His tennis had been polished in the States where he had been educated and now he was to be one of Hogan's opponents in the forthcoming exhibition matches. Y.C. like Jasmine, was a devotee of all things American.

The girl lit a cigarette and inhaled deeply 'Y.C. says there's no way Whitney can reach the top again. He's too old.'

Leah shrugged dismissively. 'About your debut at the Dynasty,' she began, not wishing to discuss Hogan again. If the truth was told she was fed-up with him. The sooner he came and went, the better.

Jasmine blew a perfect smoke ring and studied it for a moment. 'Y.C. thinks it is hilarious that I should be singing in the cabaret there. My voice isn't much good, you know.'

Leah stared back in confusion. 'But your father——'

'My father hasn't got a clue,' the girl decreed, taking another puff. 'I'm only singing to humour him, dancing is really my scene.' Her bee-stung lips firmed. 'This time I shall up-date my image. My father prefers me to be traditional, but I intend to groove. I've chosen two songs from the pop charts, Western songs with some zip, and I'm having a black suede and leather culotte suit made. I'm aiming for the racy look.'

'You mustn't do that!' Leah was aghast. It was imperative Jasmine keep a low profile, but if she appeared at the hotel resembling a fugitive from Studio 54 everyone would sit up and take notice. 'The Dynasty management need a local girl in a cheongsam to sing Cantonese melodies,' she explained rapidly. 'The oriental aspect is essential. Tourists can listen to pop songs back home, but when they visit Hong Kong they expect something completely different. They're eager to sample the Asian culture.' She suppressed the thought that Jasmine's screeching could not, in any way, be classified as 'culture'.

'I want to be with-it,' the girl said, beginning to sulk.

'Yes, but——' The intercom buzzed and Leah flicked the switch impatiently. 'What is it?'

'Hogan Whitney.'

Her stomach knotted. Why was Hogan ringing her? Saul had been dealing with him in total, so far. 'Put him on the line,' she instructed.

Violet giggled. 'He's here.'

'In Hong Kong?' She was incredulous.

There were more giggles. 'Waiting to see you,' her secretary revealed.

Leah gaped at the intercom in dismay, refusing to accept its message, then snapped her head around as the door swung open and a smiling, broad-shouldered man in a cream suit strolled in, a bubble-haired brunette tottering behind him.

'Leah,' he purred, walking forward with his hand outstretched. 'It's been a long time.'

But not long enough, she thought rebelliously, rising to accept his greeting. Her handshake was perfunctory. His strong tanned fingers closed about hers for only a second before she snatched away. Her knees appeared to be in some danger of buckling and she plopped down, frantically thumbing through his itinerary as though needing written proof that the man before her was in the wrong place at the wrong time, so he could only be a mirage. She licked lips which were suddenly dry and smoothed down the skirt of her off-white suede dress.

'You are supposed to arrive tomorrow afternoon on the Pan-Am flight. There's a press conference arranged at the airport,' she declared, aggravation hardening her tone. 'The apartment needs a final inspection, and ... and you've ruined all my plans!' She scowled at him and was furious to discover amusement at her peppery reaction flickering in the depths of his pale grey eyes. 'Everything was organised down to the last detail, and——' She broke off. 'You've grown a moustache!' she accused with an air of outrage.

Hogan ran the edge of his thumb across the dark hair bristling on his upper lip. 'Does it meet with your approval, kitten?' he challenged lazily, smiling at her from beneath lush dark lashes.

Kitten! The word billowed in her mind. Kitten belonged to the past, for only Hogan had ever called her that. Kitten meant long-gone days of love and laughter, holding hands, his lips against hers, whispers in the dark, nerve ends tingling ...

'It's the public's approval you need. What are they going to think?' she snapped, centring all her annoyance on his unexpected moustache. 'Suppose they don't recognise you from the picture on the books and posters?'

He raised a sardonic brow at her pique. 'I don't imagine there'll be any problem. Beneath the hair I'm still the same Hogan you know and love and admire.'

Leah was selecting an icy answer when she became aware that Jasmine and the voluptuous brunette were both listening to the interchange with a great deal of interest.

'Er ... won't you sit down?' she asked, realising her social graces had been knocked for six.

She rushed pell-mell from her desk, arranging chairs, ordering coffee and introducing Jasmine. She even managed a little small talk about the weather and the view. The brunette, it transpired, was called Terri and hailed from New York. For the moment Leah blotted out the reason why Terri was gazing across at Hogan as though he was the best thing since sliced bread. She recognised the look of old. She rather suspected she had been guilty of it herself, once upon a time.

After several minutes' conversation Jasmine ground her cigarette into the ashtray. 'I must go.'

Leah walked with her to the door as Hogan and Terri settled themselves in the leather chairs before her desk, sipping the coffee Violet had provided.

'Report to the band leader at the Dynasty at ten o'clock tomorrow morning, but sing Cantonese songs, *please*! And keep the culottes for another occasion,' she begged, noting how Jasmine's lower lip was blossoming into defiance. 'Believe me, you'll look sensational in a cheongsam.'

'Can it be sequinned?'

'Why not?' she agreed.

The girl was happy now and left with a smile. Taking a deep breath, Leah marched back to her desk, cultivating an air of cheerful efficiency.

'Well, Hogan, as you and Miss——?'

'Call me Terri,' the brunette intervened with a toothpaste-commercial smile.

'Well, as you and Terri are already here,' Leah began again, fidgeting with her papers. 'I'll explain what has been arranged.'

Hogan rubbed the back of his neck where the dark hair grew low. 'Terri's not involved,' he said firmly. 'She's only here as my——' He paused before allowing the word to splatter into the silence. 'Nurse.'

Leah's lips twisted as she looked straight back into his pale grey eyes. Some nurse! Nurses seldom came packaged as bosomy brunettes in orange wet-look jumpsuits and white fun fur jackets.

'Not exactly a nurse, I'm a trained physiotherapist,' Terri explained without a flicker of hesitation. 'I keep an eye on Hogan's physical fitness.'

'You keep an eye on my body,' he told her, smiling like a cherub.

'I get the picture.' Leah munched on the words as though they were pieces of cracked glass. 'What a shame you didn't warn me in advance to expect two visitors. I'm afraid you'll find the apartment is rather restricting.' She smiled briefly, a smile tinged with malice. Roger had a single bed and now that she remembered Hogan didn't like small beds, he preferred to spread himself. The prospect of his discomfort was gratifying. 'No doubt you'll manage,' she concluded with saccharine sweetness.

'No doubt we won't,' Hogan drawled with the easy assurance of a man who has thought through the situation and decided exactly what he requires. 'I stay in the apartment, Terri checks into a hotel. She can come in every day to give me the once-over.'

Leah produced a tepid smile as the ground was cut, ever so neatly, from under her. What kind of game was Hogan playing? Was Terri a bona fide physiotherapist or just the latest girlfriend? If, as Saul had said, he was one hundred per cent fit, why was a therapist required? Pretending to drink her coffee, she cast him a quick glance. He *looked* fit. His tanned skin had that sheen which is the product of supreme vitality. No doubt he still consumed gallons of milk and yoghurt. In the old days Hogan had been a flat-bellied piston of energy and from the stretch of the physique sprawled across from her, it did not appear as though much had changed.

'Would you fix Terri a hotel? I'm sure she'd like to

get over there and unpack,' he prodded when Leah continued to wallow in her thoughts.

'Yes, *sir*!' Suddenly she was furious with him, resenting the way he had deliberately put her in the wrong. He had goaded her into believing the girl must be his lover, but now she wasn't so sure. Reaching for the phone, she rang the Dynasty and swiftly arranged a room, speaking in clipped tones which were intended to portray the competent businesswoman. Terri looked suitably impressed, but Leah noticed a slight quirk tugging at the corner of Hogan's mouth. Ignoring him, she asked one of the trainees to help Terri down in the lift with her luggage and to find a taxi.

'See you later,' Hogan smiled as the girl departed. When the door had closed, he swung back to Leah. 'What a low suspicious mind you have, fancy imagining Terri and I are living in sin!'

Stamping down on her temper, she gave her coffee cup the benefit of an intense scrutiny and after a moment raised her head. 'Your exhibition matches are scheduled for the day after tomorrow, bang slap in the middle of the Chinese New Year holiday. You'll be pleased to hear that the response has been terrific. All the tickets have gone for the afternoon and evening matches, and only a few remain for the eleven a.m. session.'

'Three matches in one day?' he demanded, a muscle tightening in the tanned column of his throat.

'I thought it best to get them over with all at once, then you're available for interviews et cetera.'

With one swift surge Hogan rose from his chair and slammed down his cup and saucer on her desk. She started at the sudden clatter.

'Do you think I'm computer-programmed?' he

demanded. 'I can't play three matches in one day, especially against guys the calibre of that Y. C. Wong. From what Jasmine was saying, he's dynamite. Hell, if he's played against all the big names in the States, he's not going to be a pushover!' Hogan began striding back and forth across the carpet. 'You should be aware of the strains and stresses I live with, Leah. What the hell are you trying to do—kill me?'

'I'm asking you to knock a ball over a net,' she said coldly, resenting the fuss he was making.

'But the catch is that I must beat every single opponent. I can't afford to lose because if I do and the word gets around, my business interests will suffer. Nobody wants a loser.' He was glaring at her with tight-lipped fury. 'There's no way I can manage three sessions.'

She squashed a twinge of alarm. 'You must, I've arranged everything.'

'I don't have to jump through your hoops,' he snarled, pacing before her like a caged beast. 'So you can damn well *un*arrange it all.'

Pink-faced with righteous indignation, Leah began to protest. 'Look here, I'm helping you to——'

He gave her no chance to finish. '*You're* helping me! I know damn fine your only loyalty is to Spencer Associates. You don't care a toss about me as a person, I'm just black figures on the balance sheet as far as you're concerned.' His anger showed in the tense angle of his jaw. 'You don't promote, you *exploit*! You and Saul both.'

Leah clutched at the edge of her desk, fingers whitening. 'No one forces you to allow Spencer Associates to handle your affairs, which they do very profitably, so don't complain. If you can't stand the heat, get out of the kitchen,' she added for good measure.

His fists clenched then slackened. 'If only things were that simple,' he muttered.

'And how would you suggest I *un*arrange the matches?' she demanded tartly.

Hogan was running his hands through his dark brown hair until it was rumpled across his brow. 'I don't care how, but I don't want to play three times in one day.' His anger seemed to be spent and he cast her a weary glance. 'Have a heart. It's not a matter of scraping to victory, I have to make minced meat out of my opponents, and in style. And I bet you've saved Y. C. Wong for the evening performance?'

She nodded, feeling guilty. Hogan was a trained professional, he would never refuse to deliver the goods without reason. He had been subjected to a heavy winter schedule, perhaps the programme *was* excessive.

'We seem to have got off on the wrong foot,' she said, with a soothing smile.

'You have, not me.'

She gestured. 'Sit down, Hogan, and let's talk about this rationally.'

'Like two sensible adults?' he asked, granting her a fraction of a grin before he reluctantly subsided into his chair.

Leah inspected her papers. 'Suppose I switch Y.C. to the morning? It'll annoy some of his followers, but that can't be helped. The afternoon guy isn't supposed to be too clever so that'll be a short session.' Out of the corner of her eye she saw him shake his head helplessly.

'Okay,' he muttered.

'Things'll work out fine.' She found it strange to discover she had more faith in Hogan's ability than he appeared to have himself. 'You've had a long journey, you must be tired. Things will look different in the morning, and your leg——'

'What about my leg?' Like a switch being flipped he was on the defensive again, his anger showing in the compressed mutiny of his full mouth.

Leah backtracked. 'I wondered if you ever have metal fatigue?' she joked weakly.

'The odd spot of rust.' He produced a grin to match the wisecrack, but the look they exchanged indicated they both realised there was more unsaid than said about that particular topic.

As they moved on to discuss his television interview and other arrangements, Leah began to feel easier. Not comfortable exactly, the vibrations between them were too intense for that, but her confidence began to reassert itself. Now her fearful imaginings about their reunion seemed foolish. She had completed the briefing and was congratulating herself on her return to commonsense when Hogan sat back in his chair and steepled his fingers.

'When did you last make love, kitten?' he asked, gazing at her across his fingertips.

Her heart thudded so loudly that she was sure he must hear it. 'What . . . what kind of a question is that?' she stammered, her composure crumpling.

Over the past three weeks she had imagined their meeting and constructed the dialogue. Her intention had been to maintain an air of sophisticated cool, but first the surprise of his early arrival with Terri, then Hogan's fury over the exhibition matches and now his outright sensuality robbed her of any chance of aloof control.

'A straightforward one,' he drawled, his enigmatic

grey eyes watching her like a cat's eyes. 'We have eighteen months to catch up on, so I thought I'd skip the preliminaries.'

'You always did.'

He shifted in his chair, nonchalantly pulling at the knee of his trousers as he crossed his legs, and his inherent sexual presence made Leah's breath catch in her throat. The remembrance of him as the man she had loved, the man she had made love to, hit her like a dagger between her shoulderblades.

'Okay, we'll do it your way,' he grinned, when he saw she was not about to answer. 'Do you have a boyfriend, Miss Morrison? How long have you been dating him? Is it getting serious? Are you very much in love?'

'That's none of your business.'

'Are you answering my first question, or the second, or the third?'

'All,' she said curtly.

'There must be some guy hanging around, you're far too attractive to be left alone.' There was an audacious glint in his grey eyes. 'Let me guess. He's a Chinese tycoon, or a diplomat, or could he be a British business executive, running one of the large trading houses out here?'

Leah knew Hogan and Glenn were destined to meet, indeed Glenn had said how keen he was to watch the tennis star in action. 'I date an Australian and he manages the Dynasty Hotel,' she bit out.

'Gawd, some beer-swilling jackaroo!' He was laughing at her. 'And doesn't he mind that for the next two weeks you'll be servicing my every whim?'

Hogan's needling was too much.

'As you pointed out, all you represent to me is a profitable transaction, so in my position as head of

Spencer Associates in Hong Kong I shall do my utmost
to make life comfortable for you, Mr Whitney,' she
declared, her voice brittle. 'I shall fetch and carry, as
expected, but as far as servicing your every whim . . .'
She refused to meet his eyes. 'No doubt the adoring
Terri will be happy to cover the areas I prefer to leave
alone.'

Her sarcasm drew a chuckle. Hogan stretched
languidly, his pale jacket falling aside to reveal the
ripple of sinewy muscles beneath a dark silk shirt. 'And
what is this Aussie like?' he enquired.

'Kind and considerate, good at his job, cultivated——'

Hogan's mobile mouth creased into a smile. 'Can he
wiggle his ears?'

'He's mature and he believes in fidelity,' Leah
continued with a withering glance.

'Which means I don't?' His humour had vanished.

'You have a tendency to be—fickle,' she said, raising
her chin and refusing to be browbeaten by his piercing
gaze. It was a renewal of hostilities, the poison
blowpipes had been raised and targets pinpointed.

'God, that's rich!' he declared, breathing fire and
rebellion. He thrust himself from his chair and in one
stride was looming over her. 'If anyone is fickle, it's
you! One minute you were swearing undying love and
the next you'd shot off to bloody Hong Kong with
never a backward glance. All the months I was in
hospital I never received a single word from you, not
even a card wishing me well.' He turned away, but not
before Leah glimpsed the pain in his eyes, the bitter bite
to his mouth.

'That's not true, I sent you flowers,' she defended.

'Like hell you did!'

She well remembered the red roses she had organised

through Saul. Hogan *had* received them because Saul had passed back his thanks, thanks which had revived her foolish hopes of a reconciliation. But those hopes had died when Hogan never broke his silence again.

'I expect your room was crowded with flowers from ... from admirers, so probably mine were lost in the crush,' she said. Hogan had the grace to look uncertain and she pressed home her advantage. 'Our affair had virtually finished by then, so what does it matter? We'd both moved on. Coming to Hong Kong was a good career move for me,' she added, attempting to sound casual.

His eyes grew cold as steel. 'You're a calculating bitch!'

Leah ignored the empty feeling in the pit of her stomach. 'Aren't you out for the main chance yourself? The only reason that you're here now is to make some money.'

Hogan stood close to the window, his hands deep in his pockets, his eyes trained on the distant skyline. 'It makes sense for me to consider my future. Tennis offers no job security, no pension. If, for some reason, I fail to measure up to the mental and physical standards required, then I'm finished and I know damn well what happens when the cheering stops. At present the one way I can make a decent living is by the promotion of my name, even if it isn't the way I would choose.' He stopped abruptly, as if he was saying more than he should and sighed. 'But I didn't come all this way to justify my actions, or to argue.'

'You're right,' she agreed with a fixed smile. 'We're making no headway, let's get back to business. What do you intend to do during your second week here? I've arranged for you to use the Health Club at the Dynasty if you wish, there's a pool and a wide range of exercise machines.'

She could see the tension ebbing from him.

'Thanks, and I'd like to play some golf if that's possible.'

'I didn't know you were a golf addict.' Surprise lifted her words. 'Saul never mentioned it.'

'Contrary to what you may think, kitten, Saul doesn't own me body and soul. I prefer to keep some areas of my life private.'

The 'kitten' hurt like a secret wound, but Leah kept her bright smile pinned in place.

'Do you play much golf?' He nodded. 'And are you good?'

'Yes.' The answer came point-blank, there was no puffy pride, it was a statement of fact. 'I took up the game after my crash because the rehabilitation programme included easy walking, and golf was the perfect solution.' He glanced down at his long legs. 'Gradually the muscle knitted and strengthened, and now . . .' Leah noticed a nerve flicker in his jaw but then he smiled, his teeth white in the sultry tan of his face. 'If you can fix me up with a round or two I'd be grateful.'

'No problem. Jasmine's father, Mr Tan, is golf-mad. You're scheduled to lecture at his club later in the week, so we can have a word with him then.' She examined her file. 'I'll switch the press conference to the Dynasty, there's not much point everyone trekking out to the airport, and I might as well make it earlier. How about ten o'clock tomorrow morning?'

'Later,' he ordered.

The unexpected harshness of his command made her swivel to him. 'Why later?'

'I need a lie-in.' He was examining the skyline again.

'But ten isn't that early, and there'll be an opportunity for you to rest later in the day. The reporters have deadlines to meet, and they'll be happier if——'

'Eleven, no earlier,' he growled. His mule-stubborn determination surprised her, but because she did not want any more trouble, Leah shrugged her agreement. Hogan reached down for her hand and against her will, pulled her upright. 'Try to understand,' he said softly. Leaning against the window, he was a large black silhouette, outlined by the dazzle of the sun.

She narrowed her eyes against the glare, not quite aware of what was happening, and it took a moment or two before she realised he had stationed her before him, his hands gripping her elbows, holding her tight. The smell of his aftershave, a memorable blend of musk and patchouli, filled her nostrils and her pulses began to flutter. Nostalgia for what had been stirred within her.

'I do understand,' she replied. 'I know the publicity machine creates pressures.'

. As Hogan moved, the dazzle of the sun disappeared behind him. He was looking down at her and Leah saw she must keep talking, for his eyes were darkening in a way which was uncomfortably familiar.

'I know that people constantly swarm around you and I'll do my best to make life easier in Hong Kong. I have your welfare at heart, that's what I'm paid for,' she added, with a touch of asperity.

His brow twitched at this blunt reminder, but his hands slid from her elbows to her waist, his fingers spreading, claiming the slender curve as he pulled her closer.

'Why did it end, kitten?' He shifted his weight, standing with muscled legs set apart and holding her against him. His grey eyes penetrated deep into her own. At the feel of his intensely masculine body, Leah became aware of a raw ache within her, an ache which was begging to be assuaged. 'Why did you break us up?' His voice was husky and disturbed.

'Don't act the innocent,' she protested, as a dizzy tornado swept up her emotions, tossing them hither and thither.

Hogan's heavy-lidded eyes were caressing her face, lingering on the fresh softness of her lips. Weakly she tried to move from him, but his arms tightened.

'Kitten!' It was half a plea, half an endearment. He bent his dark head, blotting out the sun, the sky, the entire world. His mouth met hers, the bristles of his moustache teasing her skin. Leah's eyes closed of their own volition, and a ripple of pleasure swept over her body, spreading towards her toes and fingertips, making them tingle. His mouth was burning, aggressively forcing her lips apart until he sensed her answering desire and she felt him relax. Now his breath mingled urgently with hers, and his kiss was deep and searching. Held in the steel circle of his arms, Leah didn't know whether she was giving or taking as the drugging kiss lengthened. At last she found the strength to drag her clinging lips from his.

'Hogan,' she protested.

He smiled down at her in triumph. 'You've just answered my question. There's no way you're sleeping with that guy from Down Under.'

CHAPTER THREE

HOGAN was mad, bad and dangerous to know! Despondently Leah crawled into bed that night, wishing his visit to Hong Kong was already over. At his teasing words she had leapt from him as though a high-voltage current had struck, furious at her foolishness. He was too astute, and still possessed an uncanny knack of getting under her skin. Why hadn't she learned from the mistakes of the past? Hogan was a lightweight philanderer; to allow him snatched kisses was downright folly. Their love affair had been assigned to history. It was over—*period.* By playing with her he was amusing himself, like a cat amuses itself with a mouse, but that was all. And as far as her feelings about him were concerned—her thoughts stumbled at this point. She was leery of Hogan, with good reason, for his kiss had proved the old magic was as potent as ever. Leah stared out into the darkness of her room, cursing her weakness. For heaven's sake, she thought with a silent scream, when you left him he was in the process of ripping your heart to shreds, don't let him near you again.

She tossed and turned, gradually persuading herself that the kiss had meant nothing. Hogan, too, must have realised his behaviour had been out of line for afterwards he had been correct and formal. As he waited for her to make the necessary calls to alter the time and venue of the press conference, he had lapsed into silence, and for the remainder of the afternoon had seemed a little weary and distracted. He had still been subdued when she had introduced him to Roger's tiny one-bedroomed apartment.

'I'm just across the hallway,' she explained.

Hogan swung his suitcase on to the bed. 'So if I need you, I just whistle?' he asked, with a flash of humour.

'I'm trained to come running.' She had meant to say it lightly, but it came out tart.

He slanted her a glance. 'What other tricks have you lined up for me, kitten?'

Despite the 'kitten' Leah managed to keep on her emotional feet. 'For one, entertaining you.'

A dark brow arched. 'Do you dance on the table or leap naked from cakes with tassels attached to the appropriate places?'

'Neither, but I'd like to invite you out to dinner this evening, by courtesy of Spencer Associates.' Somehow it was vital she stress that business prompted her action.

'Not tonight, Josephine,' he said, much to her surprise. 'I'll see you in the morning.'

She was on the brink of suggesting they dine together in her apartment to avoid the hassle of going out, for doubtless eating in public would involve autograph hunters and conversations with complete strangers, when she brought herself up short. She was being woolly-headed. Hogan would have plans, maybe an assignation with Terri? Hadn't he said he would see her later! Leah scolded herself for her stupidity. Nurse or no nurse, Terri was a curvaceous young lady. Maybe she didn't actually live with Hogan, but that didn't mean much.

Leah nodded a hasty agreement. 'Will you set your alarm for ten? I don't want us to be late for the press conference,' she explained. 'There's fruit and cereal in the kitchen for your breakfast. I intend to go into the office early in order to deal with the post and any emergencies. When I come back to collect you I'll bring along some of your books and promotional literature. A taxi from here to the Dynasty will take twenty minutes or so.'

'I can understand why Saul reckons you're a whizz-kid,' he smiled. 'You don't leave much to chance, do you?'

'I prefer to be organised,' Leah said primly.

She watched television all evening, determined not to keep track of Hogan. What he did was his problem! When she departed for the office next morning she scoured his door with an impatient frown. No doubt he would be fast asleep, catching up on lost time, time devoted to . . . Let him have his on-off affairs, she thought cuttingly as she waited for the lift, infidelity was not her style, nor Glenn's. Glenn was loyal, thank goodness.

By the time she had read the post and made a number of phone calls, it was after ten. 'Please would you get Roger's apartment on the line?' she asked Violet, stuffing books and brochures into a large canvas bag.

Leah pulled a white blazer-style jacket over her olive green shirt and slacks, and checked her hair in the mirror. The flaxen hair was fine and straight, and when she wore it loose, as she did at home, it swung like a shiny gilt banner, reaching halfway to her waist. For business, however, she preferred a neater style, and this morning a heavy plait hung over one shoulder, intertwined with a narrow green satin ribbon. At present her hair was bandbox smart but as the day progressed, and Leah had other things on her mind, wisps tended to drift free, framing her oval face.

'You look like a tousled madonna,' Glenn had once said affectionately, tucking a silky strand behind her ear, but that was not the image she wished to project.

After a minute or two, Leah pressed down the intercom switch. 'Have you made contact?'

'There's no reply,' Violet told her.

She clicked her tongue in irritation. 'Are you sure you dialled the correct number?'

At the giggled confirmation Leah frowned, pushing back her sleeve to inspect the wafer-thin silver watch on her wrist. Vital minutes were ticking away. Surely Hogan must be up and breakfasted by now? Her call had been intended as a last-minute reminder for him to meet her in the lobby, not a wake-up call. Now she wondered if he had risen late and was still beneath the shower?

'Ask one of the boys to grab me a taxi and I'll try the number myself,' she instructed her secretary. Leah dialled with the utmost care and perched on the corner of her desk, foot swinging with impatience. What was keeping Hogan? The number rang and rang, and when she had almost given up hope, her blood pressure rising with every dragging minute, the receiver was lifted. There was a fumble, some laboured breathing and silence.

Pure exasperation swept through her. 'Good morning!'

'Hello?' a sleepy baritone slurred.

'Hogan, it's me. Were you still in bed?'

There was a long pause, and she could almost hear him waking up.

'I must have slept through the alarm. I'm sorry.'

'So you should be! You'll have to skip breakfast. I'm taking a taxi right now, so meet me outside the apartment block in ten minutes,' Leah ordered and slammed down the telephone.

He was doing this on purpose, she decided, examining her watch at two minute intervals as the taxi battled through the crowded streets. Hogan had deliberately sabotaged her plans to make it plain *he* had the upper hand! Being late was some kind of petty power play, or revenge. Her mind flew to his accusation about her apparent lack of concern after his accident, but that had been unfair. It was not her fault if he had overlooked the bouquet she had sent. So many adoring women must have sent him flowers that he had not been able to keep track!

'Would you wait here, please? I won't be a minute,' she said to the taxi driver as he halted at the porch to the apartments, but when she dashed into the lobby it was empty. Hogan was nowhere to be seen. 'Has a man been here, European man, tall man?' she asked, gesturing wildly at the security guard who was stationed in solitary splendour behind his desk.

'No man, missie.'

Swearing beneath her breath, Leah hurried to the lifts and jabbed at the call button, tapping the toe of her high-heeled suede boot as she waited. How slow everything was when you were in a rush, she fumed. When the lift arrived it climbed at a snail's pace towards the sixth floor. The lift might be sluggish, but the fingers on her watch were not. They were racing around like Olympic runners and now the time had reached ten forty-five. If Hogan was absolutely ready and the traffic helpful, there just might be time to reach the press conference as planned. She darted out of the lift, skidding along the marble floored corridor towards his apartment.

'Why on earth aren't you dressed?' Leah demanded

when, after a moment or two, the door opened to her impatient rapping.

Hogan had just climbed out of the shower, for his hair was damp and droplets of water were trickling down his neck, losing themselves in the thick dark whorls on his chest. He was wearing a knee-length navy towelling robe and his legs were bare.

'Do you realise what time it is?' she asked, temper sizzling.

'Cut out the drama,' he slammed back, matching her fury for fury. He scowled as though she were an enemy. 'Don't start yelling at me, I overslept that's all. I'm getting ready, but don't rush me. Okay?'

'In the past you were punctual,' she grumbled, stalking after him into the apartment. 'Before you were always disgustingly bright-eyed and bushy-tailed in the mornings.'

Hogan made for the bedroom. He seemed to be hobbling. Good grief, Leah thought, he's not even woken up properly, last night must have been a hard night!

'Things change. Life is different now to what it was eighteen months ago,' he flung back over his shoulder as he disappeared through the open door.

'Huh!' Leah applied as much scathing contempt as possible to her answering grunt before stomping across to the window, fractiously waiting for him to dress.

Life *had* been different. She had worked for Spencer Associates when they first met, but at a lower level and in the name of experience had been assigned to spend a few weeks with Hogan on the tennis circuit. He had been among the top twenty world players and Saul, with his unerring eye, had singled the young man out as a worthwhile investment. When Spencer Associates offered a contract, Hogan had signed on the basis that tennis came first, and that he could pick and choose his promotional work. Already he had a handful of sponsors, but Saul rapidly raked in more. Away from the pressures of his sport, Hogan was relaxed and articulate, he was the kind of man the companies felt happy with. His dark good looks helped, too. Leah could still remember her first glimpse of him, walking around the perimeter of a tennis court with his tracksuit jacket slung casually around his shoulders like an Italian gigolo, a clutch of tennis rackets beneath his arm.

'My remit is to take charge of your travel arrangements and hotel reservations,' Leah had explained when she introduced herself and he had given a slow grin, noting her pale hair and slender curves. His undisguised approval had brought a flush to her cheeks, and she had hoped it didn't show.

'I must congratulate Saul Spencer,' he drawled. 'Providing me with my own private angel is one hell of a perk!'

'And if you need any assistance with interviews or sponsors, I'll be here.'

'You'll do your best to make my life heaven?' he had teased.

'I'll try,' she assured him.

His eyes had captured hers, sending sensual messages she could not ignore. One step had been taken on the stairway to paradise, and in the weeks which followed, wonderful golden weeks in Monte Carlo, Johannesburg, Los Angeles and Houston, they had climbed higher. The stairway led up through secret kisses, nights dancing beneath the stars, heady moments entwined together until, one evening in Hogan's bed in some luxury hotel in the States, they had reached the pearly gates. He had been a gentle but virile lover. Leah had guessed he was experienced, but had been grateful; grateful he had had the control to make the first time for her such a wonderful experience.

'I love you, kitten,' he had murmured as they lay together in purring bliss.

'And I love you,' Leah had echoed, held close in his arms.

Hogan had kissed her slowly and gravely. 'We belong together, Leah, for always.'

But he had never belonged to any woman; tennis was his abiding passion, his mistress, his wife. Leah, and the girls who came after her, made a poor second. For a while love had blinkered her from the truth. She had returned to London in a state of ecstasy. Their love was young, but it was special and she hugged it around her like a soft warm blanket. Over the following weeks they were often apart, tennis saw to that, but when they did meet, Hogan flying in for rushed days between tournaments, the world was a dizzying, technicoloured delight. She felt so alive when he was near. The sun shone twenty-four hours a day, flowers bloomed, everyone was smiling, and Leah floated on air.

'You're a wicked distraction,' he had said, giving her a playful tap on the bottom. 'After a weekend with you I'm worn out.'

She had grinned deliciously. 'But you spend most of your time in bed!'

'Don't tell my coach about that.'

A pinprick of unease jabbed through Leah's bliss. 'Does your game ever suffer?'

Hogan had reached for her. 'Which game is it

you're talking about? I reckon I'm pretty hot stuff at both.'

'Convince me,' she had demurred, refusing to allow the world of tennis to disrupt their precious time together.

With a great deal of finesse, Hogan had convinced her. Life had been a glorious rush and they were so busy filling their stolen days and nights with love that nothing else mattered. Everything was wonderful, they were young and deliriously happy. Hogan was on a winning streak. Now the newspapers were forecasting that his astonishing amalgam of vibrant muscle, nerve and animal speed, combined with an astute tactical sense would lead to great things at Wimbledon. Everything looked sunny, but storm clouds had gathered . . .

The first hint for Leah that life with Hogan was not a rose garden came when Saul arrived hotfoot from New York and summoned her into his presence.

'When were you and Hogan Whitney last together?' he demanded, folding his massive hands over his stomach, where shirt buttons were straining. Saul's size, like his voice, was on an ebullient scale.

Sensing criticism, Leah leapt to the defensive. 'Last weekend, but why?'

'He flew to see you?'

'No, as a matter of fact I went over to Paris.'

'You know he's lost some games this week?'

It was beginning to feel like an interrogation and Leah frowned. 'Yes, he told me when he phoned, but he still managed to win his matches.'

'Don't you think it's time you and he cooled it, young woman?' Saul waggled a pudgy finger in her direction. 'If Hogan is going to build up that pre-

Wimbledon confidence he needs plenty of smooth wins, not cliff-hangers.'

'He said his poor showing was a hiccup.' she protested.

'More like a downright belch,' the businessman buddha said crudely. 'I've been speaking to his coach, and he reckons Hogan's attitude has been changing over the past few weeks.' He held up a hand to quell the protestations on Leah's lips. 'Only a subtle change, I grant you, but he's not as single-minded as he used to be. And we all know why, don't we?'

'That's unfair, Hogan's had girlfriends before me,' she said uncertainly.

'Nah! He's never gotten himself *involved* before.' Saul drummed his fingers on his stomach. 'You're a bright girl, look at this objectively. He's twenty-seven years old and though he's held a place in the top twenty computer ratings for a couple of years he's never managed to pull off Wimbledon, though he's won most of the other major tournaments. This could be make or break time for him. If he wins his future is secure, his name will be worth millions, but——' he paused to make sure of her attention, 'if he screws it up, then Hogan Whitney will be added to a long list of also-rans. I admit he could still make a good living, but he wouldn't be top dog.' Saul challenged her over his bifocals. 'Do you want to deprive him of that?'

Leah knew when she was backed up against a wall. 'No,' she said.

'So let the guy be, but don't upset him.'

She felt all shook-up and unhappy inside. 'We'll talk the matter over.'

Rolls of flesh redistributed themselves as Saul slid deeper into his chair. 'Don't do that, honey, he'll only get uptight. He can be a stubborn cuss if he feels he's being manipulated.' Leah flashed him a glance which said she could understand why, but her boss took no notice. 'All we want is to keep Hogan on an even keel. Use your womanly wiles and draw back a little. Give the guy more time to concentrate on what really matters.'

'His tennis,' she muttered.

'Right on.'

Reluctantly Leah had begun a strategic withdrawal. Over the next few weeks she managed to put space between herself and Hogan by concocting a collection of excuses—phony influenza, family duties, pressure of work. She so much wanted to do the best for him that at times she became paranoid; was she pulling back too far, or not far enough? Fear began to gnaw. If she was protecting Hogan's career, wasn't she also strangling their relationship? Hadn't her boss placed her in a Catch 22 position? There were periods when she wondered if she was naive in believing Saul's assessment. He was an unprincipled rogue, to say the least, and it was entirely probable that he had some ulterior motive in mind. Other tennis aces had girlfriends and wives, and nobody charged them with causing trouble. But her relationship with Hogan *was* hot-blooded and demanding, how could it be otherwise when every moment together was hard-won.

Yet Hogan gave no indication that he was aware of her retreat, and that was the most damning thing of all. Could he truly care for her as she cared for him and still be immune to her withdrawal? He was not on her emotional wavelength any longer, how could he be when he accepted her evasions so casually? Something shrivelled inside Leah when he carried on with their relationship as though everything was hunky-dory. There was no alternative but to settle for the status quo, and because Saul did not raise the matter again she had assumed he was satisfied, but she had been wrong . . .

Without warning her work pattern changed. Instead of being London-based, she was given assignments in the States and spent time moving from one European capital to the next, filling in for executives who were ill, or on leave. She was lucky to be chosen for the training was invaluable, and at first she had been flattered that Saul had such faith in her ability.

'You're destined for the top, honey,' he had boomed when he spelled out the assignments. 'Soon you could be running a branch of your own.'

When she discovered that Hogan had mixed feelings about her sudden rise in the public relations world, Leah felt a flood of relief. So he *did* care, after all!

'This career woman stuff means I can hardly keep track of you,' he had complained and Leah had snuggled up to him, delighted to hear his masculine grumbles.

'What about your tennis?' she had taunted, happy now.

'That's different.'

'Sexist!'

Hogan made a bite for the end of her short straight nose. 'It's normal for men to be aggressive careerists, but five-foot-three go-getters scare the pants off me.'

'I had noticed.'

'Metaphorically speaking, of course.'

Her eyes danced. 'Of course.'

'The trouble is, I'm a sucker for long blonde hair and breasts which fit into my hands.' He had ducked to avoid a sharp clip to the jaw.

'Sexist,' she said again.

'What I'm *not* a sucker for,' he said, not joking now, 'is us being apart.'

Leah had bit into her lip, hesitating. With a flash of insight she realised her sudden spate of travelling was too much of a coincidence. Saul had not been content with her self-imposed separation, and he was deliberately hammering a wedge between them. Should she tell Hogan what was happening, how she had already been forced to draw back? Dare she risk trouble? Hogan's tennis was going well and despite her fears *he* did not seem unduly perturbed about their relationship. But if she revealed that her boss was interfering in their private lives, he would be livid. Hogan already viewed the older man with mistrust, calling him a con-man, so his reaction would be explosive. Wimbledon was approaching and when the pressure built Hogan had a hair-trigger temper to match his hair-trigger reflexes. On court he kept his cool, but off it . . . No, a bust-up at this stage was unthinkable. Leah had changed the subject, but later in the evening when Hogan had told her of an appointment with Saul the next day, she had felt a stab of apprehension.

'Why does he want to see you?'

'So he can congratulate me on my performance so far.' Hogan did not add 'of course', but his tone implied it.

Leah had glanced at him sideways. He enjoyed his success, and why not? Grand Prix tennis was a painful stretch of mind and muscle, and she knew the sacrifices he made. Next morning she had discovered she was to be sacrificed too . . .

The sound of a door slamming brought her back to the

present. Hogan sauntered across the living-room, a
brown leather jacket slung nonchalantly over one broad
shoulder. He was wearing biscuit-coloured trousers and
a rollneck sweater in a paler shade. Lips thinning, Leah
examined her watch. They were destined to be well and
truly late for the press conference. The taxi driver
would have grown tired of waiting, so now another cab
would need to be waylaid. She marched towards him,
ablaze with complaints.

'Simmer down, kitten,' he smiled forestalling her, and
in ostentatious slow-motion donned the jacket.

'The name tag's sticking up at the back.'
Automatically Leah raised a hand to push the label
from sight, but her movement froze. 'Maybe you leave
the manufacturer's name on show as part of their
advertising campaign?' she asked facetiously.

'The logo is on my chest.' He edged his jacket aside
to expose a tiny badge.

Leah let him obliterate the offending tag himself. 'I
imagine if you removed all the clothes you're promoting
for your sponsors you'd end up stark naked,' she said
acidly.

'Are you imagining me stark naked?' Hogan was
grinning, his eyes full of devilish glee. 'Tut-tut, but how
about vice versa?' Seductively he ran the tip of his
tongue across his lower lip as he looked her up and
down, mentally undressing her.

She flushed crimson. 'Are you ready?' she demanded,
furious about the ease with which he could reduce her
to a quivering mass.

He collected up a large sports bag and collection of
tennis rackets. 'This afternoon I'll be warming-up,' he
explained when she looked curious. 'Can you find me
some competition?'

'I'll try, now come on!'

Leah was forced to admit Hogan possessed a dexterous touch where the media was concerned. She had imagined their tardy appearance would be greeted by sour faces, but she had forgotten his deadly charisma. He strode into the press conference like a conquering hero, smiling and returning greetings, and within minutes, as Saul had prophesied, everyone was eating out of his hand. Hogan was totally in control, whether detailing the injuries he had suffered from his car accident or enumerating his daily fitness programme. Leah knew he must have recited the same facts *ad nauseum* throughout the many countries he had visited, but he still managed to produce an unruffled air of enthusiasm.

'Firstly there's an hour of exercises, press-ups and so forth. Afterwards I lift weights.' He flexed a jokey bicep and everyone chuckled. 'Then it's running and tennis, tennis and more tennis.'

'What do you do during your leisure hours?' a Chinese reporter wanted to know.

'I exercise in bed,' he replied, with a broad wink.

The fact that he was grinning towards Leah when he spoke made her bristle. Okay, so his double entendre had brought a roar of laughter from the press as intended, but there were limits! She scowled at him. She knew damn well the men envied him and the women were wondering how they could catch his eye. He was living up to his image in full, only it was no longer an image. Beneath the gloss was more gloss, for Hogan had apparently become the playboy sportsman Saul required. Leah was surprised when his mood changed and he responded seriously to questions about the future.

'I don't like gazing into a crystal ball, and I have drawn up no blueprint,' he said. 'At present the overwhelming concern is to work myself back into competitive tennis.'

There was a babble of questions as the journalists tried to draw out what kind of goal he had in mind, some timed commitment, but Hogan verbally elbowed aside the demand for predictions.

'Is this comeback for real or just a money-making exercise?' one of the wilier reporters asked.

'I never apologise about money,' Hogan replied, with no semblance of a smile. 'I enjoy good living as much as the next man. But no, the comeback is for real, and it's not spurred on by the need for either money or glory. I'm a professional and tennis is my business. When I'm out on the court I'm not there to hear the crowd yelling or to tot up a run of healthy figures on my bank account, I'm there to play the perfect game. To me tennis is an art form and my satisfaction comes from getting it right. And that means winning,' he said, almost as an afterthought.

The press conference ended when Hogan rose to his feet and declared that time was passing by and now he must stop talking tennis and start playing tennis. After a round of cheery farewells the reporters drifted away.

'I'm meeting up with Terri for a physio session. I rang earlier so she'll be waiting,' Hogan said, collecting up his gear.

'You might have warned me,' Leah protested, feeling a surge of unreasonable annoyance that he had dared to make his own plans.

'I'm warning you now,' he drawled, raising a mocking brow at her petulance.

He was intent on having his own way, Leah realised as she marched beside him through the broad thickly-carpeted corridor towards the bank of lifts, but how was she to do her job if he was sweetly indifferent to what she had in mind? Hogan halted to sign a scrap of paper for a blushing teenager, while she stood by, seething. He was so pleasantly polite that Leah wanted to grab one of his rackets and break it over his dark head, anything to disrupt his composure.

'And what about lunch?' she asked, when they resumed their journey. She tried for lightness, but knew it hadn't come off.

'I'll order something in Terri's room. If I eat in public there could be interruptions. This afternoon I shall work out on the courts.' He hitched his bundle of rackets further under his arm. 'It would help if you could get Y. C. Wong to practise with me.'

'But today's the eve of the New Year holiday, he'll probably be busy,' she retorted, stubbornly refusing to ease Hogan's path. Why should she jump when he said jump?

He caught hold of her wrist, forcing her to a halt. 'You can do it for me, kitten, *please*.' He was gazing unsmilingly down into her eyes. 'Help me, Leah.' She heard an unexpected throb in his voice, a note of raw need. His strong fingers tightened on her arm and he drew her closer. The nearness of him had Leah's heart spinning. 'You were the best thing that ever happened to me,' he said in his slow-fuse voice, 'and——'

Whatever was coming next she never discovered for the rackets beneath his arm began to slide and suddenly they were both clawing frantically, striving to halt the unwieldy load before it tumbled to the ground. Leah found herself clutching at the sleeve of his leather jacket with one hand, the other spread across the hard muscles of his chest, muscles which moved beneath the fine cashmere sweater. Together they straightened.

'Can't fall any further,' he grinned, grey eyes flicking over the debris on the carpet.

She returned his grin and suddenly she was caught up in a spell. It was like the old times, just she and Hogan together without a care in the world. She laughed, nudging the heap with the toe of her boot. 'Who cares about a few lousy rackets?'

'Who does?' His words were low and throaty.

Slowly he stretched out his fingers to caress the smooth contour of her jaw, his heavy-lidded eyes brooding on the tasty fullness of her mouth. An errant flaxen strand floated against her cheek, and he smiled, catching it between his fingers and smoothing the hair with solemn intensity. Leah sensed a latent power in his muscled physique, the taut grip of hesitation. Words were struggling inside him. He was tempted to say something, something important, but on the edge of speech he drew back.

'Leah!'

Her head jerked up at the sound of an intruding voice. Glenn was marching towards them, his face alive with pleasure.

'What's happened here?' he asked, indicating the windfall of rackets. He grinned at Hogan and took hold of his hand. 'On behalf of the Dynasty Hotel chain, and myself, I'd like to welcome you to Hong Kong.'

Hogan took the hearty welcome in his stride, but when Glenn turned to greet her, kissing her cheek, Leah found it difficult to produce the correct air of casual affection. Still sizzling from the emotional electricity Hogan's touch had created, she was off-balance. Fortunately Glenn did not notice anything amiss and blasted off with a stream of questions, predictable ones which she had heard Hogan answer earlier in the day, but which he now treated with the same urbane civility.

'I'd like to have a look at the courts,' he said in response to the Australian's assurance that the entire resources of the hotel were at his disposal.

'The courts it is,' Glenn smiled.

Leah escaped to telephone Y. C. Wong with a feeling of relief. He expressed immediate delight at the chance of a practice game and promised to be at the hotel within the hour, and although it was good news, Leah had to quell a tiny stab of pique. Y.C. had sounded so *flattered*. He was probably rushing around gathering up his tennis gear and singing at the top of his voice, overjoyed at the thought of meeting Hogan. Glenn had been equally as enthusiastic, and it rankled. Indeed she was annoyed to discover the Australian was still lavishing praise when she joined them outdoors.

After a painstaking inspection the courts were awarded Hogan's seal of approval which Leah found consoling, but her satisfaction was shortlived for when they reached the Health Club, designated as the scene for the matches should the weather be wet, Hogan's brow furrowed savagely.

'Far too cramped,' he decreed, expert eyes scanning the pine-planked gymnasium.

'Tennis is played here on a regular basis, see the floor is marked out,' Leah protested, her spirits sinking.

'With spectators?' he drawled.

'No, but we shall open up the dividers like this,' said

Glenn, hurriedly clicking his fingers at the attendant to unlock the folding wall.

'Even with that out of the way there isn't sufficient space. It's the length that is vital,' Hogan insisted.

The Australian marched off. 'There's adequate length,' he shouted back as he strode out the distance.

'Sorry, but no.' The way Hogan kept his voice deliberately flat warned Leah he was about to erupt.

'We can manage,' soothed Glenn, Micawber-like.

'No way,' growled Hogan. 'Do you know the speed of a tennis ball when it's served? If one should ricochet and a spectator is hit there'll be a nasty accident. The hotel could be sued, and so could I.'

Glenn came back to where Hogan and Leah were waiting in the centre of the gymnasium. 'Can't you softpedal on the serves?'

Hogan gave an incredulous grunt at this suggestion. 'I play tennis to win, and how the hell am I supposed to do that if I'm on pins about whether I'll break someone's false teeth or smash their spectacles to smithereens?'

Leah broke into Glenn's laughter. He might find the reply amusing, but he was the only one that did. 'So what happens if it rains?' she asked in a small voice.

'We cancel.' Hogan's husky drawl had a biting edge.

Her green eyes widened in distress. 'Cancel!'

'You'll have to kneel on your prayer mat, beaut, and ask the gods for sunshine,' quipped Glenn, smiling guilelessly down at her.

She gritted her teeth. Usually he was on her side, but now he had taken his cue from Hogan and was nonchalant. How dare he be nonchalant about cancelling the matches when it meant certain disaster! She had spent days and days on organisation, hundreds

of tickets had been sold, and now Glenn was casually
tossing around the prospect of cancellation as though it
meant nothing. This was all Hogan's fault, she decided,
balling her fists. He was intent on disrupting her life in
every possible way, but his disruptions were not yet
over . . .

'I've arranged for us to dine here this evening with a
journalist from a local magazine,' she told him as they
left the gym.

'You might be dining out, kitten, but not me,' Hogan
said firmly. 'If I'm expected to win three sessions of
tennis tomorrow I need sleep, lots of it. I'll have a
room-service snack with Terri, and then go back to the
apartment and to bed.'

Leah was tempted to ask if the order of his timetable
was not somewhat muddled, but managed to restrain
herself. Whether Terri functioned as a genuine physiotherapist she neither knew, nor cared!

'Reschedule the dinner for later in the week,' he told
her, being noticeably patronising. 'You're a respected
lady with a winning smile, I'm sure you can make
suitable apologies on my behalf.' He grinned at the fury
sparking in her eyes. 'Naturally, if you wish me to
grovel in person——'

'No, thank you!'

'I'd like to invite you to join Leah and me for a meal
at Chinese New Year,' Glenn intruded, with the air of
someone intent on diverting nuclear warfare.

Leah frowned at him. Why did he have to interfere
and include Hogan in what had been intended as a
private occasion?

'That sounds like fun,' Hogan replied, casting a
sardonic eye on her. 'May I ask my keeper if I'm
allowed to attend?' He bent his dark head to hers.

'Please, Miss Morrison——' he began mockingly.

She gave him a plastic smile. 'Do join us.'

He swung to Glenn. 'Leah pours oil on the waves before I walk on them,' he explained.

'Shouldn't we include your—your companion in the invitation?' Leah asked, with a trace of vitriol.

'A physiotherapist travels with me,' Hogan told the Australian, who nodded his understanding.

'Bring her along, and suppose we include Y. C. Wong? Jasmine is to be in the cabaret that evening so perhaps he would like to hear her.'

'He can always smuggle her out under a blanket if the guests start throwing things,' Leah muttered.

'I've just heard her rehearsing and she's not that bad,' Glenn said jovially.

His good humour and benevolence were maddening. 'Jasmine's voice is pathetic,' she insisted.

'She looks better than she sings,' he admitted with a smile.

The trio broke up, Hogan taking the lift to Terri's room, while Leah and Glenn went to the entertainments desk.

'Every last ticket sold for the tennis,' the receptionist announced in reply to his query.

'Imagine all those irate ticketholders if it should rain!' Leah bleated, unable to banish the horror. 'What will we do?'

'Reschedule for another day.'

'And suppose it rains *then*!'

'Don't cross your bridges,' Glen coaxed, giving her a farewell hug.

How could she *not* cross her bridges? Leah wondered as she journeyed back to the office. Public relations work depended on planning ahead, on detailed

organisation, but also on being flexible, a little voice
inside her head reminded her. It was not the end of the
world if the matches were rained off, or was it? She
decided to lay on contingency plans, just in case.

Violet was rushing around like a mad thing when
Leah reappeared, full of more giggles than usual
because New Year was imminent. The letters dictated
that morning were neatly typed way ahead of time, and
when Leah had added her signature Violet whisked
them off, only to return minutes later bearing a large
white cake box.

'Special for New Year,' she announced. 'You try, you
try.'

The two trainees came in, closely followed by a group
of Chinese executives and their staff from offices above
and below. All Violet's cronies appeared to have been
invited and in no time the room was buzzing. Even
Pauline deserted her groundfloor reception desk and
arrived to gossip. Leah didn't know who or what was
being discussed, but there were several glances in her
direction and she began to wonder. Not that she cared
too much for the mood was festive, everyone was
laughing and talking nineteen to the dozen. To
accompany the sweet pastries and fondant cakes,
someone produced a bottle of brandy, a Chinese
favourite, and tumblers were handed round. When the
first bottle was upended, another miraculously
appeared.

Leah staggered back to her apartment that evening,
distinctly woozy. A girlfriend telephoned to suggest a
get-together but she was too full of cake and brandy
and cried off, using Hogan as an excuse. For a while
she dozed on the sofa, and later, when the mists of
alcohol lifted, she ate an apple and switched on

television. The programmes were geared to the four days of Chinese New Year which stretched ahead and one interviewer, when listing events over the holiday, referred to the next day's tennis at the Dynasty. Leah crossed her fingers. She intended to rise at the crack of dawn, firstly to check that the weather was fine, and secondly to make certain Hogan was up and about in good time. Over her dead body would he be late tomorrow!

She kept half an ear cocked for noises in the corridor to indicate he had returned, but heard nothing. Should she telephone Terri and check that he had left at a decent hour? Leah's pulse rate quickened. Despite his comment, she was *not* Hogan's keeper and, besides, she had no wish to hear first-hand that he had decided to spend the night playing doctors and nurses!

She awoke early, leaping from her bed to fling wide the curtains. The sky was a clear sweep of blue, not a single cloud in sight, and the sun looked as though it was here to stay. 'Thank you, thank you,' she said to no one in particular, as an avalanche of relief swept over her. Now her contingency plans could be stuffed into the waste paper basket, where they belonged. Her good mood was such that when she had showered and dressed she decided to wake Hogan and suggest they breakfast together. It was barely eight-thirty when she rapped a brisk tattoo on his door. Leah was convinced he would still be in bed and was forced into a backward step of surprise when the door was promptly opened.

'Good morning, kitten,' Hogan panted.

She had obviously interrupted his exercises for he was clad only in brief yellow satin shorts, a white towel slung around his neck. The tanned muscles, glistening with sweat, made Leah's heart race a little faster and it was difficult not to stare at the rhythmic rise and fall of his chest.

'Er . . . I came to see if you'd like some breakfast,' she managed to say, forcing her eyes up to his face. Suddenly she was short of breath, too.

Hogan seemed very pleased with himself, and with her, for he began running on the spot, his grey eyes happily wandering over her shapely figure in white tee-shirt and jeans.

'I must admit the best place for me is stretched across you,' he said, gulping in a breath.

Leah glanced down at her shirt with its portrait and 'Watch a Champion in Action' slogan. 'You like it?'

'I like it—them,' he adjusted with the smile of an impudent schoolboy. 'That 3-D effect is terrific, it sure beats advertising on the side of buses. Have you ever considered selling space, because if so I'd like to put in a couple of bids.'

'Be good, Hogan!' she warned, remembering how his sexual teasing had frequently developed into something more.

'No, I wouldn't like any breakfast, thank you. I've already eaten,' he told her, still smiling.

His good humour proved infectious and Leah found herself smiling too. 'What time did you get up?' she asked.

'Seven.'

Her eyes widened. 'So early?'

'I've been working out. As soon as I've showered and you're ready, I'd like to get down to the hotel for a spot of practise.'

'Your wish is my command,' she said, standing to attention.

Hogan's professionalism was impressive. At the back of her mind Leah had wondered if his matches would turn out to be so much ballyhoo. She knew that on exhibition tours players often grew careless, sloppy habits were formed because it was difficult to produce a flow of adrenalin, and understandably so. But the moment Hogan stepped on to the court that morning, she could see he *cared*. He was giving the public value for money, and using the matches to hone his expertise. Leah was aware of the extra mental ingredient he possessed—his fantastic determination to win, and she realised that regaining his position at the top of the international tennis tree was no pipe dream. It could be reality.

Seated among the crowds in the sunshine, she was reminded of the other occasions when she had watched him play. The moustache was new, and rakishly attractive, but apart from that little had changed. His responses, developed after a lifetime's practice, were still swiftly accurate, his concentration still as complete. You could explode a cannon beside Hogan when he was lining up a serve and he would never hear it. Elbows on her knees, chin cupped in her hands, Leah watched him. How well she remembered that oddly appealing twine-toed stance before he smashed the ball at his opponent. He had been right about not playing in the gymnasium she saw that now, for a goodly proportion of his serves were aces, whizzing like bullets to thud against the far link fencing. In a confined space the balls would have been deadly.

Between sessions he was relaxed. Leah tried to rush him away from the court, anxious for him to escape the clamour of the crowds, but was forced to wait while he signed autographs, chatted and posed for pictures with eager fans.

'I don't know how you cope, she exclaimed when eventually he allowed her to steer him up to the hotel room which had been set aside for his use. 'You must be worn out and yet you're so damn polite!'

Hogan slumped into a chair, sweat pouring from him. 'It's my job, kitten.'

'Day-in, day-out, you answer the same questions. People used to make a fuss before ... before your accident but even in Hong Kong it's akin to mass hysteria,' she complained.

'Don't forget it's transient. Crowds can turn nasty if you offend them. One day they love you, the next they'll lynch you.'

'But in your case there'd be a cavalry of women waiting to gallop to the rescue,' she commented drily.

'Speaking of women, where's Terri?' he asked, looking round.

'I'll go and find her.'

Leah was unable to keep the frost from her voice. Hogan appeared to be as close to Terri as he had once been to her, and the realisation hurt. She knew it was illogical but the thought of the brunette closeted away with Hogan between his tennis sessions annoyed her. After all, he had never needed a personal physiotherapist before!

She decided to skip the evening match, so once Hogan appeared on the floodlit court she set off in search of Glenn and a little comfort. Chinese New Year was a busy time at the hotel, and he had been able to watch only a few minutes of the morning match before being called away. Ever since the manager had been tied up with business matters and was poring over a wad of reservation schedules when she entered his office. Glenn yawned and stretched, pushing the papers aside as he rose to greet her.

'Everything going okay on the tennis scene?' he asked, winding his arms around her.

Leah rested her blonde head against his shoulder. 'Fine. The evening performance should be a walkover. Y. C. Wong retreated with his tail between his legs this morning, so I imagine this challenger will be dealt with in double quick time.'

'I hope Hogan doesn't finish the match too swiftly. People want their money's worth.'

Leah moved away to look out of the window. Far below the tennis court made a dazzling rectangle of light in the hotel grounds. 'He only plays to win, he won't give any points away. But when he wins, he wins in style. He'll keep his fans satisfied.'

Glen ordered some coffee and they idly discussed the day, reaching the conclusion that the tennis matches had been a resounding success from everyone's point of view.

Leah glanced at the clock on the wall. 'I'd better go down, the session must be nearly finished.'

'I'll come and take a look myself.'

But when they reached the court they discovered that only four of the proposed five sets had been played.

'Hogan's taking a long time,' she protested as Glenn slid in beside her on the wooden benching.

He gave a thumb-jerk at the scoreboard. 'Seems this evening's adversary is not the pushover you imagined.'

'Hogan must be turning the match into a nail-biter on purpose,' she decided, upturning her previous ideas.

Each man had won two sets and now the score was three-two to Hogan's Chinese opponent. Leah watched askance when Hogan proceeded to lose the next game. Eyes trained on him, she leaned forward. His movements were sparse, he was no longer ranging across the court as he had done earlier in the day. Leah frowned, her blood running cold. Hogan was in trouble, deep trouble.

CHAPTER FOUR

'SOMETHING must be wrong,' she whispered into Glenn's ear.

She was prickling with unease, her eyes narrowed as she focused on the athletic figure beneath the glare of the floodlights. Poised on the balls of his feet, Hogan was crouched forward, swaying from side to side as he anticipated the next service. Beneath his sweat-sodden sports-shirt, the muscles of his shoulders were like stone. His attitude was one of intense concentration, but was that all? Couldn't she detect a do-or-die glitter in his eye, wasn't he fighting against the odds?

Glenn scorned her fears with a careless toss of his hand. 'He's fine.' Hogan smashed away a lob to win the point, then took the next with a particularly vicious backhand. 'There you are, he's just stringing the guy along,' the Australian smiled as the scoreboard lit up to indicate Hogan's victory. Despite a run of flawless aces which left his opponent standing, Leah continued to fret, sucking anxiously at a fingertip. Couldn't Glenn see that Hogan was not covering all the angles as he should? But when she started to voice her fears, he laughed. 'You'd not be daisy-fresh if you'd been playing tennis all day,' he chided.

Another game to Hogan and Leah started to relax. She had not seen him in action for nearly two years, perhaps he had changed his style. She relaxed further when he proceeded to turn the next few minutes into a feast of tennis, displaying acutely-timed forehands

73

which skimmed across the baseline, some impudent
dropshots and a flurry of backhands with a tricky top-
spin. The crowd were delighted and when the last
dazzling delivery had been made they rose en masse,
applauding wildly.

'Game, set and match to Hogan Whitney. There's
nothing wrong with him,' Glenn announced, clapping.
'Like you said, he was making the match an occasion.'

Leah wasn't convinced. As Glenn departed for his
office, she began pushing a way on to the court where
the crowds were milling around. When she reached
Hogan he was busily signing his name on programmes,
sun-visors, even a plaster cast on someone's arm. The
excitement he generated was tangible, everyone wanted
to see him, touch him, foist their attention upon him.

His eyes lit up with relief when he saw her and he
stretched out a hand. 'Let's go,' he said.

Easing a path through the throng was tricky. More
and more autograph books were thrust beneath his
nose, more and more fans appeared to clap him on the
back and praise him. Progress was slow. Beneath his
tan, Hogan was pale. A towel was slung around his
neck and from time to time he dabbed away the sweat
which trickled unendingly down his jaw. Beneath the
merciless lights the lines of exhaustion were sketched
plain around his eyes, and a nerve jumped un-
characteristically in his temple.

'I must get away,' he muttered to no one in
particular, and continued to inch towards the haven of
the hotel, signing his name as he went.

Leah was grateful for the security guard Glenn had
thoughtfully stationed at the door of the room reserved
for Hogan, for groups of teenagers had tailed them and
there was the babble of conversation outside in the

corridor. Hogan collapsed into an armchair, sinking his head into his hands. He looked drained and, watching him, Leah couldn't help feeling guilty. She, alone, had been responsible for arranging his punishing programme.

After a moment he glanced up, anxiety furrowing his brow. 'I didn't desert the fans too hastily, did I? Fatigue can be interpreted as disdain, and that's the last impression I want to give, but I had to get away.'

'You behaved perfectly,' she assured him, pouring out a tumbler of orange juice.

The ice clinked temptingly against the side of the glass as Hogan gulped it down. Wiping his moustache with the back of his hand, he gave her a weary smile. 'Thanks.' Gingerly he bent to rub at his thigh, frowning down in worried concentration. Beneath the mat of sweat-dampened hair on his leg Leah could see silver-white scars, the legacy from his crash.

'Does the leg trouble you?' she asked.

'*No*, it damn well doesn't!' he snarled right back.

His unexpected anger stung. She had spent her entire day, a day when most people in Hong Kong were on holiday, looking after his needs and when she had asked a simple caring question he had lashed out. What right had Hogan to be short-tempered? All he had to worry about was his tennis, and he had proved his supremacy three times today in that direction. No, it was people like her who had the hassle; they dealt with his itinerary, his travel arrangements, his income, his tax, his health— especially his health!

'I expect you require Terri's services?' she enquired with arctic coldness.

He plucked ineffectively at the damp dark hair

clinging at the nape of his neck. 'I didn't mean to shout,' he apologised, sidestepping her question.

Leah tossed her head. 'That's what I'm paid for. I'm Spencer Associates' walking, talking punchbag. Far better you take your temper out on me than spoil your image with the ever-loving public!' She knew she was being unjust, but did not care. 'I'll contact Terri,' she announced, flouncing across to the telephone. If Hogan decided to spend the night with his toothpaste wonder, that was his choice. She couldn't care less!

'Let's just go home. I'm shattered,' he said quietly.

Leah was tempted to send him off alone in a taxi while she returned to Glenn's goodnatured presence, but ethics stopped her. Like it or not, while Hogan was in the Colony he was her responsibility and if, as a major money earner for Spencer Associates, he should hint to Saul that her attentions had been lacking she knew darn well who would be fed to the lions.

'Whatever you wish,' she agreed icily.

Hogan's spirits revived once he had showered and changed and now he appeared intent on charming her. He was using all his masculine attractions to wheedle his way back into favour, she thought ruefully, but try as she might, Leah could summon up little resistance. By the time they reached the apartments she had thawed completely and he was amusing her with a cheerful informality which seemed appropriate in the circumstances. His harsh denial that his leg could be troublesome had only served to warn her that it *was*. She knew him too well not to recognise evasions of the truth, but the subject had been dropped. He was walking normally but when he caught her sneaking a glance at his thigh, now encased in beige corduroy jeans, his eyes darkened so stormily that she could not find the courage to raise the matter again, so it hovered between them like a skeleton at a feast.

When they reached his door Hogan slumped his bag and rackets on to the marble floor and patted his jacket pockets. 'Where's the key?' he muttered as he searched, but after a moment he raised his head and gave her a wry smile. 'I've locked myself out, kitten. I remember slamming the door shut behind me when we left this morning and unfortunately the key is still on the kitchen table. Do you have a spare?'

Leah let out a breath of exasperation. 'I'm afraid not, but the porter downstairs should——' She stopped short.

'Well?' He was slouched against the wall, arms folded. Perhaps it was a trick of the light, but there were dark rings around his eyes and the skin was stretched right across his high cheekbones. He looked much older than his twenty-nine years.

'Well, he's not on duty right now because of the New Year holiday,' she explained, becoming businesslike. 'Give me a few minutes to go downstairs and discover what standby arrangement has been made. Presumably there is a set of spare keys in the building.'

Hogan shifted his weight from one foot to the other. 'Could I wait in your apartment? I'm just about ready to topple over.' She risked a quick glance at his leg. 'General exhaustion,' he snapped, quick to take offence. 'Don't forget that thanks to you I've been running around like a scalded cat ever since seven o'clock this morning!'

Leah let him into her apartment and stomped away. She was tired too, Hogan did not have a monopoly on such things. The mislaid key annoyed her and she scathingly decided he should have been provided with a

nursemaid, never mind a nurse! It was difficult to
discover anyone who knew anything, but at length she
was told that the spare keys had vanished with the
porter and were presumably languishing at his home
over in Kowloon. Her temper began to bubble. The
porter did not have a telephone and the thought of a
long taxi ride, searching for his home at this time of
night, did not thrill her. She hurtled back along the
corridor towards her apartment, composing a tirade of
descriptive sentences which would leave Hogan in no
doubt at all as to his rock-bottom rank in her esteem.
Pampering him might be her job, but enough was
enough.

She powered into the living-room, flames of fury
leaping from her nostrils, and was taken aback to
discover the room was empty.

'Hogan?' Her voice echoed in the stillness of the
night, then there came a tired murmur. Following the
sound Leah made for her room and discovered Hogan
stretched full out on the bed, fast asleep. She glared at
him, her yards and yards of unused condemnation
circling fruitlessly in her head, then she gave a mock
growl of despair as her anger fell away. He looked
exhausted. Hogan asleep was a defenceless little boy, his
lush lashes heavy on his cheeks, strands of dark hair
straggling across his brow.

A little spasm of the heart made her quiver. How
many times had she seen him asleep, felt his sweet
breath warm on her skin, sighed blissfully as he moved
closer to her in the deep of the night? Oh God, she
wanted that again! Leah pressed knuckles to her lips,
struggling to banish her foolish longings. There was no
future in wanting Hogan, there never had been. Tennis
was his true and only desire. So he had told her he

loved her and possibly had, in his fashion, but the emotion had been flawed, too weak to last. She swallowed hard, remembering that dreadful morning when she discovered the truth—that Hogan was prepared to sacrifice everything, even her, in the name of tennis.

Saul was in London on one of his flying visits and Hogan had gone into the office at his request. When lunchtime arrived, Leah had deserted her desk on the floor below and wandered up to wait. They had arranged to lunch at a nearby Italian restaurant and she inspected her watch, hoping the meeting was about to finish for time was limited.

'Those two have been going at it hammer and tongs for the past hour,' the receptionist whispered when Leah entered the outer office. She nodded towards the heavy oak door. 'Sounds like Mr Spencer could have met his match. Hogan can give as good as he gets, can't he? They've been growling at each other all morning. I don't know what the trouble can be, but something has surely upset the apple cart.'

Doom settled on Leah, like a black eagle alighting on her shoulders, its claws piercing her flesh. Saul Spencer had not reached the pinnacle of the public relations world by sitting back and letting things happen. Saul was a manipulator, and at present he was determined to manipulate her and Hogan. Beyond the door she could hear her boss stressing a point, rumbling on and on.

'I'm off to lunch,' the receptionist said gaily, gathering up her jacket and bag. 'I should read a magazine if I were you, you're in for a long wait.'

Leah gave a laughing shrug of acceptance and sat down in one of the black leather armchairs. For a few minutes she studied the splashy abstracts hung around the walls, then inspected her watch again. Time was drifting by. She knew Hogan would endeavour to bring the meeting to a hasty close and when the handle of the door jerked down, confirming her faith in him, she gave a wide smile. He was joining her. But when the door was opened a few inches, the movement stopped.

'How long have you been living, sleeping, eating tennis?' Saul's voice boomed. He answered his own question wearily, as though the matter had been chewed over at length. 'Since you were a boy. And what haven't you won? Wimbledon. And does it matter?'

He sounded about to answer that question too but Hogan, just behind the door, was quicker.

'Yes, it bloody well does! I *need* Wimbledon and you know it.'

'Then look at this objectively.'

Leah's smile was obliterated and her expression grew tense. Whenever her boss said, 'Look at this objectively', he really meant, 'Look at this my way, the *only* way'. She could hear him cracking his fingers and realised those could be her bones he was pretending to break.

'It's a matter of priorities,' he said loudly. 'Tennis or girls.'

'Girls' sounded as though Hogan was out carousing with a different female every night and Leah scowled. She waited for him to protest that there was only one girl in his life, someone devoted and understanding, who was no danger to his career, but he didn't.

'My sport comes first, as always,' Hogan drawled.

'So wise-up,' demanded Saul heatedly.

'I have,' the younger man barked, matching anger for anger.

'Leah's a pretty little thing, but she's a career woman.

She isn't a camp follower. She wouldn't be prepared to sit on the sidelines knitting for the rest of her life.'

'I know that.' Behind the door Hogan was still barking.

Leah's heart missed a beat. Her career was important to her, but Saul was distorting the issue.

Her boss changed tack. 'I don't ask you to live like a monk. You're a redblooded male and you're young. A few affairs on the side won't upset anything, in fact they'll help to relieve the tension.'

'Like Leah does?' If Hogan was joking, it didn't sound funny. His cryptic reply lit fires of despair and resentment. So that's what I am, she stormed, a tailor-made divertissement, on a par with a stiff whisky or a day on the beach!

'That girl is capable of lousing up your career,' Saul continued, hammering her into the ground with every word.

Silence. Stand up for me, Hogan, she implored, half inclined to barge into the office in her own defence. But she was eavesdropping, though by chance. Her instinct warned she would do better to walk away and ignore what had already been said, but feminine curiosity kept her motionless. Like it or not, her life was on the line and she was intrigued by the opportunity to learn Hogan's views on their relationship, for better or worse.

It was worse.

'No-one louses up my career, but *no-one*,' he said fiercely.

'So don't get in too deep,' warned Saul.

'I don't intend to. Just leave matters, Saul. This is *my* life and I'll run things *my* way.'

'Marriage can wait,' her boss blundered, immune to the inherent threat in Hogan's voice.

'Marriage is the last thing on my mind right now,' he cut in quickly, too quickly.

Stricken, Leah closed her eyes. The subject of marriage had not been raised for although they had known each other several months, their actual time together had been brief. They were still getting to know one another. And yet surely it had been understood that one day they would exchange golden rings and be man and wife? No relationship could stand still and when they had daydreamed of their lives together she had presumed ... Too much, it seemed.

'Marvellous,' Saul boomed, and there was a palpable change of mood. 'Cut loose. Kick up your heels, have a fling, several flings if you wish, but never forget what comes first.'

There was a rasp of dry laughter. 'Do you take me for a fool?'

Saul chuckled. 'No siree.'

The door was pushed closed, and Hogan must have returned to her boss's side for the murmur of voices continued. Plans were being discussed, plans which did not include her. Crushed, Leah sat for a long time, her fingernails biting deep into the soft leather of the chair. In a few short sentences Hogan had dismembered her world. She realised now that she had never stood a chance of becoming his leading lady, that place was held by tennis while she was back in the chorus line.

In a daze she made for the lift and ended up in the nearby square, where she sat on a form and stared at the lunchtime joggers and gambolling children with blind eyes. Silly fool, she had taken so much for granted. What should she do? What came next? Tackling Hogan with the accusation that he did not love her enough was puerile. In any case, she was too proud for that form of attack. If she ended their affair herself she would, at least, emerge with her dignity intact. Blinking back the tears, she thought how much she loved him, but it was unrequited love, and pathetic. She was damned if *she* would be pathetic. Leah fumed and fretted in turns, not knowing what to do. When she returned to her office there was a note from Hogan. He apologised for missing their lunch date, hoped she understood, and had now had to leave for an appointment with his accountant. He looked forward to seeing her this evening.

But when they came face to face, Leah had resolved nothing. She was jittery, more so when she discovered Hogan was his usual easy self. He chatted as she poked at the lamb chops roasting in the oven and although she laughed at his jokes she felt a great deal of sympathy for those about to face a firing squad. She knew she was destined to die inside when he told her about his meeting with Saul and its deadly ramifications, yet wasn't it preferable to have the matter out in the open? Didn't she want a clean break? Half of her was terrified he would announce that their affair had to end, while the other half awaited his words with a morbid eagerness.

Hogan showed no signs of serious intent, or guilt, or hidden thoughts; indeed he sprawled beside her on the sofa like a happy panther on splendid terms with the world. How she managed to survive dinner, she did not know. She was a far better actress than she had realised and managed to respond to his conversation, intelligently discussing this and that until finally she could bear it no longer.

'What did Saul have to say?' she blurted out, conscious of having issued an ultimatum.

Hogan thrummed his fingers on her wrist. 'Good news, he's fixed up a long-range deal for me involving a variety of options. Much depends on my showing at Wimbledon, but even if I lose there'll be product endorsements, personal appearance tours, that kind of thing.'

His casual air of pleasure dismayed her. 'And if you win?' she said sharply.

'Then there's all that *plus* the chance of making an exotic travelogue series for television, *plus* a "teach yourself tennis" strip to be syndicated throughout the world, plus, plus, plus.' He chuckled happily. 'The pluses go on for ever. By the way,' he added, and Leah froze, aware the crunch had come, 'I'm afraid our brief time together will be even briefer over the next month or so, kitten. My training schedule is pretty drastic before Wimbledon and I'll get into trouble if I don't knuckle down.' He squeezed her hand. 'We'll make up for it afterwards.'

'Yes,' she gulped.

'You do understand?'

She nodded, unable to speak. Oh yes, she *did* understand! Hogan was too kind, or was it too cowardly? to make a declaration that would terminate their friendship for once and for all. Instead she was being eased out, given the push in the gentlest possible way.

'Don't look like that,' he murmured.

She raised her chin. 'Like what?'

'Bereft.'

The love they made that night was aggressive. Leah knew her feelings were too intense, tinged with the violence of despair, but she had no choice. Caught in a maelstrom of confusion, loving Hogan and hating him, she realised this would be the last time. Desire had never throbbed so deeply when he kissed her, his hands and mouth wandering over her until they were both panting, flesh fused into flesh. Whispering his imperfect love, he took possession body and soul, moving inside her, dominating her until she felt she had no more substance than a handful of dust scattered in the breeze.

Next day he had rejoined his coach and as the Wimbledon countdown started the disciplined training became relentless. Superficially his phone calls were as ardent as ever, but to Leah they were a sham. Wounded pride forbade her from flailing him with his faults, yet she could not summon up the willpower to end their relationship herself. When Saul sent her to work in the States for a week or two, she was grateful. Now there were only brief trans-Atlantic telephone conversations when Hogan said he loved her and she echoed the same empty words. By the time she returned Hogan was living in a remote country hotel, his time segmented into tennis, exercising and sleeping. There could be no more stolen nights together.

Due to inter-company moves the Hong Kong post fell vacant and when Saul suggested she go out there on a trial basis Leah could think of no reason to refuse.

'Aren't you staying to watch me at Wimbledon?' Hogan had protested, hurt apparently oozing from every pore.

'I'll come back when you reach the finals,' she had promised, not quite knowing why.

With some misgivings she had flown east, but had been so trammelled by the pressures of coping with a new job in a new country, in a different environment, that Hogan had reached the quarter-finals before she had had time to draw breath. When she had phoned to

congratulate him, she had been told he was out
celebrating and when she read the newspapers, she
knew how. A large photograph of him, arm-in-arm with
a Brazilian heiress, was slashed across the sports page
and the accompanying article left little doubt that he
had taken Saul's advice and was having a fling. Within
days Hogan was in the papers again, but the headlines
now; *Tennis Ace Mangled on Motorway* the caption
screamed. He and his heiress had been speeding along
in a fast car when a tyre burst. The car had slewed,
bouncing against a bridge support and somersaulted
wildly before coming to rest on the sloped grass verge.
Hogan's thigh had been shattered and his dream of
winning Wimbledon equally so.

The instant Leah heard of his crash she forgot their
problems. Her place was with Hogan, she loved him,
that was all that mattered. Without hesitation, she rang
the airport, despairing when the day's London flights
proved to be fully booked. After some strenuous
hustling she managed to reserve a seat on the first flight
out next day, and rushed back to her apartment to
throw some clothes in a suitcase. As an afterthought she
remembered to ring Saul, currently in London, to
explain her impromptu departure.

'But Hogan's life isn't in any danger,' her boss had
shouted, half a world away. 'Sure his leg is in one hell
of a mess, but he's still managing to flirt with all the
nurses and pinch their backsides.'

'I want to see him,' she said determinedly, unamused
by her boss's bluff comment and the way the scenario
had somehow shifted.

'But does he want to see you, honey?' Saul allowed
the question to hang in the air. 'He and that South
American dolly are a hot number. She's in the same

hospital, but by some fluke of fate she only suffered minor abrasions. I understand she's constantly at his bedside, keeping him amused.'

Leah went cold inside.

'Don't fly back right now,' her boss continued. 'Leave it a while, let matters ride. He won't run away, he can't.' There was a macabre guffaw.

In a flurry of indecision, she nibbled at a fingernail. 'Then I'll send him some flowers and a letter,' she decided.

'Mail your note to the London office and I'll arrange to have it delivered to the hospital, along with a bouquet.'

Her trip had been postponed, only for days she had persuaded herself at first. But Hogan began to recover and the days turned into weeks. Saul reported back his thanks for her flowers, but that was all. Snippets of news surfaced, praising the Brazilian girl's devotion to the young tennis star in his hour of need. Hogan never wrote, never telephoned. Leah cancelled her flight.

A sudden movement made her start, and she laughed at herself when she realised Hogan had merely flung an arm above his head in sleep. Idly she wondered what had happened to the heiress for in due course her bedside seat had been taken by a model, a girl tennis player, then an actress. She had stopped following the gossip columns after that.

With a sigh she eased Hogan's shoes off his feet and pulled the bedspread over him. He was still wearing his jacket and trousers, but she refused to start undressing him! Leah switched out the light and softly closed the door. In the living room she opened up the folding sofa, arranging it into a bed. She had slept there before when her parents had visited Hong Kong, and when friends came to stay, so it was no calamity to sleep there again. In the morning, however, she would chase up the key and shove Hogan back into Roger's apartment where he belonged. She showered as silently as she could, though she suspected it would take an atom bomb to wake him. Tucked up in bed, she could only manage a few drowsy minutes pondering over the day's events before she, too, fell fast asleep.

A sudden noise punched through her consciousness and Leah sat bolt upright. Pale grey light shimmered behind the curtains, so it had to be morning, but what had woken her? Arms outstretched, palms flat on the mattress, she blinked away the drifts of sleep and cocked her head to one side, listening.

'Oh God!'

When she heard Hogan moan she was out of bed like a shot, wrapping her happicoat over her satin nightdress and automatically lifting her fall of flaxen hair free from the collar. On opening the bedroom door, she stared. Hogan was spreadeagled on the floor by the side of the bed, floundering beneath the frilly, pale pink counterpane, the bedside lamp on his chest, its shade rolling at his feet. He looked big and awkward and furious.

'Enjoy your trip?' she asked sweetly, trying not to laugh.

He was struggling to disentangle himself from the electric cord with one hand, and rubbing his head with the other.

'No, I didn't dammit!' he snarled, thrashing about ineffectively.

'How the mighty are fallen in the midst of the battle,' Leah simpered, leaning against the door, hands on her hips as she watched him. She couldn't help smiling.

'Cut out the Biblical quotations,' he snapped. 'Help me.'

'You can get up by yourself,' she said, suddenly aware that she was clad only in a low-cut nightgown and a short happicoat which barely covered the essentials. In those circumstances she trusted neither Hogan, nor herself, one single inch!

'I can't,' he said simply, lying there.

'Come on, Hogan, don't try the little-boy-lost approach, it isn't your style.'

'I can't get up,' he repeated. 'It's my leg, it gives way sometimes.' His eyes were glittering, daring her to show even a flicker of satisfaction, but Leah knew when to gloat and when not to gloat.

'Then allow me to assist you,' she said, walking forwards. The table lamp was gathered up and replaced on the bookshelves, the counterpane tossed back on to the bed. He must have woken in the night to make himself more comfortable, for he was bare chested, his shirt and jacket lying in a distant corner.

'Thanks,' he said, pushing himself up on to his elbows. 'Now, if you would stand astride and give me both your hands.'

For a moment Leah wondered if this was some kind of trick. She knew from the past that Hogan had a wacky sense of humour and a strong sex-drive. One swift pull and she might find herself lying on top of him! But that nerve was leaping in his temple, and there was no hint of humour in the grim set of his mouth. She did as he instructed, steadying herself as he pulled against her. By using his good leg to provide the required strength, he managed to slither back on to the edge of the bed where he sat, rubbing his thigh and wincing.

'Shall I call the doctor?' she asked, now knowing his pain was genuine, and feeling anxious. Hogan did not complain about trifles.

'*No!*' He rounded on her, but his anger was momentary and he caught hold of her hand as she made to move away. 'Forgive me,' he pleaded with a half-smile. 'First thing in the morning the thigh muscle is often a little weak.'

'And how often do you fall over?' she queried, obeying the pressure of his fingers and sitting down beside him.

He shrugged. 'I don't. I have an exercise routine which allows my leg time to strengthen gradually, but this morning I . . . I.' He shrugged again. 'I guess I forgot.'

'Yesterday's tennis wouldn't help, the programme was too heavy.' Feeling guilty, she squeezed his hand without thinking. 'I'm sorry, I didn't fully understand.'

'There is nothing to understand,' Hogan cut in swiftly. 'Once I'm on the move I'm physically as good as ever I was. When I see what I can do in the gym, measure my recovery rate, I'm technically perfect. Well, nearly perfect,' he amended with a lopsided grin.

Leah frowned at him. 'But yesterday evening . . .?'

'I was tired, that's all.'

She could see he was determined to rebuff any shortcomings. 'And what is Terri's opinion about your weak thigh?'

'She doesn't know and you mustn't tell her,' he ordered with stern aggression. His fingers tightened around hers like a steel band. 'Promise me this will be kept between the two of us, Leah.'

'But Terri is a trained physiotherapist, I presume?'
She was unable to resist a dig. 'Isn't she employed to
keep an eye on your body?'

'Do you know who employs her?' he demanded.

'You?'

He shook his head vigorously. 'No, Saul does. She
isn't charged to my account on the sly, I've checked.'
He gave her a quick glance. 'Recently I tried to opt out
of some of the travelling. The problem with my leg is a
minor irritant, but I decided that maybe a week or
two's rest might clear up the trouble for once and for
all. I told Saul I needed a break.'

'But he couldn't bear for the cash register to stop
ringing!' she commented drily.

Hogan's smile did not reach his eyes. 'How did you
guess? We exchanged some pretty harsh words. In the
end I compromised, which is how I come to have a
week off in Hong Kong once my promotional work is
finished. To my surprise Terri appeared on the scene,
though I've yet to discover whether he's provided her
because he feels some general physiotherapy might help,
or——'

'Does Saul suspect something is wrong with your
leg?' she asked warily.

'Good God, no! He's the last person I would confide
in,' Hogan's brows met in a frown. 'So I can't
understand why he wants Terri to travel with me. Mind
you, she's good at her job.' He gave a mirthless grunt.
'But knowing Saul's fetish for promoting my super stud
image it could be the health angle is irrelevant and that
she's just window-dressing.'

'So she isn't one of your . . .' Leah's voice trailed off
into a thin line.

'She's damn well not!' he barked, furious at the

assumption. 'Okay, Saul points girls in my direction, but I still retain my rights of refusal. I don't leap on everything that moves.'

'Don't you?' said Leah tartly. 'That's not the impression you give.'

'Kitten, if I'd had half as many women as Saul maintains I'd be in a little jar on a laboratory shelf by now.'

'But there have been several,' she insisted, determined to plug the point.

Hogan sighed. 'At times I curse my predictability. Saul introduces a blonde and if she appeals, I give it a spin. But since you left me I haven't found any woman I can stand for more than a few weeks at a time. I know when I first meet them that they're only cannon fodder.'

There was a certain humour in his description, and she hid a smile. 'But you could ask Terri to be discreet,' she persisted. 'Perhaps she might suggest some treatment which would help.'

'Don't you know who she is?' he asked, and she looked blank. 'Terri is Saul's niece, and I don't trust that overfed walrus as far as I could throw him. Do you?'

'No,' she admitted. Leah was innately honest, even her allegiance to her employer came second to the truth.

Hogan spread his hands. 'So I don't know if there is any tie-up between the two of them and I have no intention of taking chances.' He gave her a level look. 'Are *you* intending to report back to the big boss?'

She sat up stiffly. 'No, I'm not! And I had no idea Terri travelled with you, or that she's related to Saul.'

He gazed at her in silence as though assessing how far her reply was genuine. 'Heaven be praised, don't tell me you are innocent of his devious doings!' he said, tongue in cheek.

'I'm not in collusion with him against you, if that's what you mean,' she retorted, affronted by his jibe. Being coupled with Saul Spencer made her feel distinctly uncomfortable.

Hogan's expression grew bleak. 'That's exactly what I do mean. I thought I could trust you, I hoped I could. Do you understand why I need to keep all knowledge of the weakness in my leg strictly between the two of us?'

'Because Saul will start applying pressure if he hears any rumours.' Leah said flatly.

He nodded. 'He'll discover some way of squeezing publicity out of the situation. Hell, it's only a weak muscle, but if Saul suspects something is wrong he'll emphasise the sob-story aspect. Crippled tennis star grapples with agonising fate,' Hogan announced, as though reading a headline. 'I don't need that kind of schmaltz. I don't want any sympathy, dammit! All I require is to be left alone to make the climb back to Grand Prix tennis. And without the press breathing down my neck every inch of the way. It's bad enough having to cope with endless questions about my car crash and time in hospital. That experience is like a bloody albatross around my neck, all thanks to Saul Spencer! He was in seventh heaven when my leg was rebuilt and he's never stopped plugging that angle.' Hogan finished his tirade with a weary sigh, and she noticed he was easing his fingers over his damaged leg again.

'You should rest,' she said, and plumped a pillow behind his back as he obediently swivelled to stretch out on the bed. 'Didn't the surgeon issue any warnings about how much wear and tear the muscle will stand?'

He patted the bed beside him. 'Sit down.' Reluctantly Leah did so, and he smiled at her, draping an arm casually around her shoulders. 'The leg is supposed to be as good as new, if not better,' he said. 'I was warned to avoid sudden jolts and knocks, which I do, but that's all.'

'But did you explain to the surgeon just how demanding your fitness regime is?'

For a moment he pretended to be engrossed in flexing his knee, then he admitted, 'I guess not.' When she started to protest, he laid long tanned fingers across her lips, silencing her. 'I have a little stiffness in the mornings, that's all.'

'And is it ever swollen?'

He arched a teasing brow. 'Do you mean my leg?'

'Yes! Is it swollen now?'

Experimentally he eased his fingers across his corduroy covered thigh. 'A little,' he admitted.

'Would you like me to take a look?' Leah was wracked with worry.

The arm around her shoulders tightened as he rocked with silent laughter. 'Kitten, you want to undress me? You're just the same as all the other women.'

Her eyes blazed green fire. 'Like hell I am!'

'No, you're not.'

Hogan had stopped laughing. His grey eyes became sombre and he slowly pushed his hands through her silken hair, cupping the back of her head as he pulled her towards him. Their lips met gently, tentatively and Leah caught her breath, drowning in the nearness of him. His mouth moved over hers, nibbling and caressing, feathering kisses until she shuddered and her soft lips parted. Hogan eased her down beside him on to the pillow, murmuring words of love, his mouth mastering hers so completely that Leah became aware of a need screaming through her system. Why did she never feel this urgency with Glenn? Why did he never make her senses spin, her limbs turn to liquid honey? As Hogan's large hands slid beneath the happicoat to caress the pouting swell of her breasts, a ripple of desire surged through her. Beneath the fine satin of her nightgown twin peaks were pressing into his hands, hands which stroked and fondled until she stirred against him, needing more. But she shouldn't be doing this! She murmured a complaint, some incoherent protest that became a whimper as he edged aside her robe and the nightgown beneath to bury his head against the perfumed valley of her breasts. His mouth was hot and urgent, moving across her skin to deposit fevered kisses, his tongue flicking and flaming her burning flesh.

'You taste so good, you smell so good. Lemon verbena always reminds me of you. Do you remember those wonderful nights?' He broke off to rub his lips across the tight thrust of her nipples and Leah whimpered again. 'Kitten, no woman has ever satisfied me like you do. You're the only one who has ever made me ...' His husky voice slurred as his mouth resumed its avid journey.

Leah's blood pulsed molten hot as he opened his lips on her straining breast and she held him close, her hands roaming across the bronzed width of his shoulders, rediscovering the bulging muscles she remembered so well. She gave a sharp intake of breath at the pleasured torment of his mouth, and Hogan's hand went down, caressing.

'Darling,' she gasped, rocking against him, rolling her

golden head from side to side on the pillow at the sure steady stimulation of his hands and his mouth.

Somewhere, far away, there was a jingle-jangle, a ringing. Leah murmured for him to listen but he paid no attention, preferring to ignore any distraction as he devoted himself to coating her body with kisses, long slow kisses which made her sigh and wriggle closer. The ringing persisted, on and on until it penetrated her conscious thought. She pushed against his shoulders, and suddenly she was in earnest, her hands flailing against the suntanned muscles.

'There's someone at the door,' she told him. Hogan raised his head and stared at her. 'The bell's ringing,' she said.

'Let it ring.' He bent to kiss her again, but there was a shout of Leah's name in the corridor which would have awoken the dead. 'Hell, it's Terri,' he growled, swearing viciously as Leah pulled herself from his arms and crawled off the bed. 'What on earth does she want?'

She smoothed her happicoat back into a respectable position.

'You!'

CHAPTER FIVE

IT seemed to Leah that the rest of the day was spent hurtling from one place to the next like a jerky-limbed character from a nineteen-twenties movie. Stalling like mad in order to allow Hogan time to coax his leg back into action, she welcomed Terri into the apartment, babbling at top speed while she opened the curtains, made toast and coffee, folded blankets and sorted out her makeshift bed. The tale of the mislaid key was embroidered into an hilarious saga, though she took particular care to say that Hogan had slept in the bedroom while she had occupied the sofa. Remembering his reputation she wondered if Terri would believe her, and then didn't know whether to feel grateful or deflated when no eyebrows were raised and her account was taken as the gospel truth.

When Hogan made his entrance, she glanced furtively at his leg and was relieved when he winked a secret reassurance. She rushed to shower and dress, and after a hasty breakfast departed to locate the missing key, leaving the morning's physio session about to start. Fortunately the porter and keys were at home, and Leah accomplished the round trip to Kowloon and back in double-quick time. Now able to gain entry to Roger's apartment, Hogan disappeared to shave and change, emerging in a dark suit and damson silk shirt just as she was beginning an anxious countdown.

'We're due at Selvam's in twenty minutes,' she

explained, gathering up her schedule and heading for the lift, Terri and Hogan a step behind.

'What is Selvam's?' asked Terri.

'A department store which is promoting Hogan's books and tennis gear.'

The brunette screwed up her nose. 'How come the store is open when today is a holiday in Hong Kong?'

'Because Selvam's is owned and operated by Indians who aren't too fussed about this particular New Year. They have another one of their own.'

'Sounds a perfect chance to gain a few dollars extra at the expense of the Chinese,' Hogan commented drily.

Leah nodded agreement. 'But it's the other way round when the Indians shut up shop for their festivals,' she pointed out.

'So some souvenir shops may be open today?' Terri mused. 'I'm booked on a sight-seeing tour later this morning and I'd just love to pick up a few mementoes on my way round.'

'Like unattached gentlemen?' asked Hogan.

Leah wasn't quite sure whether or not he was joking, but Terri had no hesitation in bursting into peals of laughter. ''Bye,' she said, waving cheerfully, her white teeth flashing as she strode energetically off along the street.

As they waited at the kerbside for a taxi, Leah pulled a face at the mist which was hanging over the island like a damp grey veil. 'It's not a good day for seeing the sights.'

'Don't worry, Terri will adore Hong Kong. She has an enormous capacity for enthusiasm, rather akin to her Uncle Saul's,' Hogan said scathingly.

Tourists and locals alike were sauntering through the

elegant shopping precinct when they arrived; some marvelling at bright shop windows dripping with gems, others pausing to haggle over cut-price cameras and radios.

'Very impressive,' Hogan said, eyeing a spectacular indoor waterfall which plashed, seemingly from the heavens, into a boulder-strewn pond where pink and white waterlilies floated.

The marble-pillared entrance to Selvam's lay ahead, bordered by chic window displays of fashions and leather goods. Leah realised that groups of people were monitoring their approach, and when a European woman tapped Hogan on the shoulder to request an autograph, a murmur ran through the shoppers. Suddenly they were surrounded. She was grateful when Mr Selvam arrived seconds later and took charge.

'Stand aside,' he ordered the crowd, windmilling his arms energetically. 'Please allow Mr Whitney to reach my department store.' The Indian was a short, pot-bellied man with large dark eyes which rolled dramatically as he declared lavish appreciation that the tennis star had deigned to grace his domain. 'So delighted to see you, so delighted,' he repeated, sitting Hogan behind a desk and shooing the spectators into a haphazard queue.

The sportswear department of his shop had been adapted to the promotion. Glossy posters were pinned to the walls, there were blow-ups of Hogan receiving gold cups, a television was running the latest of his tennis training videos and grinning assistants were stationed behind glass counters piled high with Hogan Whitney books and tennis gear.

'I'm getting writers' cramp,' Hogan complained when he had been signing copies of his books for a full half-hour, but it took another thirty minutes before the crowd slackened.

Still murmuring his delight, Mr Selvam whisked them off to a private room where refreshments were provided.

'I watched your match yesterday evening,' he smiled. 'How cleverly you played. The other chap was allowed to sniff victory and then you whipped it from beneath his very nose. Tremendously exciting!'

'I'm pleased you enjoyed the match,' Hogan smiled, his grey eyes swerving from Leah's when she subjected him to a knowing frown.

In painstaking detail Mr Selvam started to relive the previous evening and twenty minutes later her heart was sinking. He seemed intent on discussing every single shot, with no end in sight. The schedule was tight, their next appointment loomed, but even Leah's noticeable references to her watch could not deter the Indian's recital. She was itching to leave and when he broke off, to offer more tea, she launched into hurried apologies and farewells.

'I'm surprised you didn't provide roller skates,' Hogan drawled, as she tip-tapped beside him on her spindly heels, rushing him across the shopping precinct and waving for a taxi.

Her lip curled. 'All you have to do is turn up and smile. *I'm* the one who made the arrangements and who is responsible if anything goes wrong!'

Lunch with the director of an international company which sponsored Hogan was next on the list, and an abundance of green lights and sparser traffic than usual meant they arrived only minutes late. As usual, Hogan was welcomed with open arms, and Leah stood in the background catching her breath. She was amazed to

discover that what she had expected to be an intimate
family gathering was, in fact, a full-scale bonanaza. All
the 'top' expatriates appeared to have been invited and
she was thankful she had decided to wear her navy-blue
Italian silk suit, rather than the casual Hogan tee-shirt
and jeans. Middle of a misty February day or not, there
were metallic cocktail jackets, feathered pillbox hats,
plunging necklines. The director's wife, a ferret-faced
lady with freckles and a plummy accent, took charge by
slipping a bony arm through Hogan's and steering him
out on to a covered terrace where a pride of middle-
aged women were pawing at the ground. Leah's fate
was to discuss the weather with the director's uncle, an
Old Colonial gentleman who rocked towards her as he
spoke, nearly asphyxiating her with whisky fumes, and
who was determined to recount every typhoon which
had hit Hong Kong since World War Two. By mid-
afternoon he had droned as far as the seventies, and
with profuse apologies Leah made her escape, explaining
that she and Hogan must depart to meet a deadline at
the radio station.

'I was just about dying of boredom in there,' she
complained as they retreated.

'Me, too,' said Hogan.

'You!' She was surprised for he had spent the entire
period flirting with goggle-eyed females.

'Well, at least you only had one admirer to cope with.
I was terrified in case one of my group elected for an
après-lunch gangbang!'

She chuckled at the image of Hogan going down
beneath a rugby scrum of ageing ladies. 'You'd manage,
that famous stamina of yours would shine through.'

'Like hell.'

While Hogan was being interviewed, churning out the

same old answers to the same old questions with an easy smile, Leah shared a cup of tea with Sue, a friend who worked there as a disc jockey.

'And when are you and Glenn getting hitched?' Sue questioned, frowning down at her fingernails.

Leah looked puzzled. 'We're not.'

'Does he know that? The guy's crazy about you, but it's unfair to keep him at arm's length for ever.'

'I have no intention of doing that,' she said indignantly and laughed to show Sue how mistaken she was. 'Glenn and I have a beautiful relationship.'

'And?'

She lifted and lowered her shoulders. 'And what?'

'And what happens next? If you don't want him why don't you step aside. You've been dating him for more than six months, you must know whether it's serious or not.'

'I don't.' The admission was guilty, almost inaudible.

Sue gave a grunt of impatience, and changed the subject.

The light was fading fast when they returned to the apartments, each going their separate way to change for the dinner date at the Dynasty. The evening was to be a formal affair, the men in dinner jackets, the women wearing cocktail dresses. Leah laid out a softly-clinging dress of chalky-green chiffon which was one of Glenn's favourites. The dress had a high jewelled collar, but precious little in the way of a back.

As she showered and shampooed her hair, she considered her talk with Sue. Obviously the girl fancied Glenn and her questions had been self-interested, but too much on target nonetheless. For weeks now Leah had suspected Glenn was working up to a proposal.

Indeed, there had been one or two occasions when she had deliberately switched the conversation to a lighter vein, but why was she avoiding the issue? Combing through her wet hair, she stared at her mirror image. She was fond of Glenn, he was kind and sociable, good fun, but . . .

Her full lips firmed. Whatever she felt for Glenn, it was not enough. How could it be when she had been on the brink of giving herself to Hogan that very morning? She pressed her palms against her forehead in despair. Was Hogan destined to be her first and only love? Would she never meet another man capable of making her heart blossom, whose touch had her melting like snow in the sun? Yet a man who would put her first?

Leah started to blow-dry her long hair. If she was honest she had compared Glenn with Hogan right from the start. She compared *every* man with Hogan, dammit! The Australian had won points for his selfless devotion, because he was always good-tempered and due to the fact his nature was sunny and open. Why Hogan scored, she did not quite know. He was a complex man, self-assured, self-contained and with a temper capable of exploding like a powder keg. Yet he was also loving, tender, thoughtful. Leah sighed, wondering if she had ever truly known him.

In retrospect their affair had been too intense, too rapid, too physical. They had travelled too far, too fast. Glenn was content to follow the pace she set, Hogan never had been. A dry little laugh escaped her lips. What a dewy-eyed fool she had been, and still was! The drier buzzed ineffectively in mid-air. She had to admit that where she was concerned Hogan possessed his personal supply of dynamite, he always had and, she suspected, he always would. Wielding the drier like a

demented Japanese warrior, Leah came to the conclusion that if she was to survive the next two weeks it
was vital to avoid any further emotional entanglement
with Hogan. She knew exactly how vulnerable she was
and armed with that knowledge surely she would be
able to resist him. Wouldn't she?

Rapidly she finished styling her hair, and her eyes
took on a determined glint as she came to a second
decision. This evening she would explain to Glenn
that their relationship had drifted off-course and now
it was over, finished, kaput. Her capacity to blinker
herself from the unpleasant or inconvenient dismayed
her, but tonight she would be honest with him,
though she knew he would be hurt. And hurting him
would hurt her . . .

'Pie in the Sky', some wit had named the restaurant
which covered the top and thirty-sixth floor of the
Dynasty Hotel. True, a delectable steak pie did appear
from time to time, but the menu was more generally
awash with smoked salmon and oysters and costly
western delicacies. During Chinese New Year, however,
the ambience was oriental. Large round tables with
revolving centres replaced intimate tables for two,
scarlet tubes of imitation firecrackers decorated the
walls and there were the inevitable red and gold Chinese
lanterns. The discreet murmur of conversation now
swelled to a noisy mix of the trailing Cantonese lilt with
a variety of European languages.

Glenn was waiting when the high-velocity lift shot
Leah and Hogan skywards, and minutes later Terri and
Y. C. Wong arrived. A choice window-side table had
been reserved and when orders had been taken for
aperitifs, everyone relaxed and admired the view.

'It's like fairyland,' Terri exclaimed, clapping her hands in delight.

The day's mist had cleared, leaving the night sky crystal-clear. Far below and across on the island, the streets resembled ribbons of coloured light, and ferries scuttled like golden beetles on the inky waters between. Vertical signs of Chinese characters shone in red and blue neon, while every skyscraper carried a slogan, some flashing on and off like Christmas trees, others constant night eyes.

'Hong Kong is magical,' the American girl sighed.

'Did you enjoy your sight-seeing?' Leah asked.

Terri gave a wide white smile. 'It was yippy-yoo! I met up with a guy from Wisconsin and we decided that the East just blows your mind. We've compiled an itinerary of what we need to see tomorrow, so after I'm through with Hogan——' he pulled a face at this offhand dismissal, '——we're visiting Ocean Park. We couldn't fit that in today, but we did visit——' She promptly embarked on such an extravagant tale of the wonders she had seen that Hogan, beside her, appeared in some danger of choking on his Bloody Mary.

Leah risked him a glance, but quickly lowered her eyes when his amused gaze met hers. No further reference had been made to the rash incident in her bedroom, and she was beginning to wonder if it had meant anything to him. He had been pleasant and co-operative all day, but if he felt a special attraction for her, he was careful to keep it hidden. She was certain everyone they had met, including Glenn and Terri, had no suspicion that the morning had begun so dramatically. But perhaps Hogan didn't consider making love to her was dramatic any more . . .?

'You sound to have had a great time,' Glenn

commented when the brunette ran out of superlatives. 'And how about you two?' he asked, his smile linking Leah and Hogan.

Hogan grimaced. 'Leah's hoicked me over Hong Kong at top speed, showing me off to the populace whether they like it or not. It would be far easier if she had me stuffed and mounted on the wall like a trophy and then everyone could file past at their leisure—and mine!'

Her green eyes sparked rebellion. 'Do you imagine I'm rushing around for the sake of my health? Well, I'm not. I'm promoting your interests! And much as the idea of stuffing and mounting you tempts me——' She broke off as a wave of laughter engulfed the table for everyone had read a double meaning into her outburst. For a moment she struggled to maintain an icy disdain, but the hoots of laughter were contagious and she dissolved into giggles.

Glenn placed his hand over hers. 'I should hope not,' he said, when order was finally restored.

Hogan kept silent, but the intensity of his expression warned her that he *did* consider their lovemaking had been dramatic. The grey of his eyes had deepened, and he was sitting still, too self-contained, too remote in his own thoughts, a faint smile flickering on his lips. After that she avoided him like the plague, not risking a glance in his direction for she was terrified she might see desire in his grey gaze, and if she did might she not feel desire also? Strenuously she addressed her conversation to everyone but Hogan. She was relieved when menus were handed round and Y.C. Wong took charge, discussing the Chinese cuisine and explaining the more obscure items with patriotic relish.

'Sea slug!' shrieked Terri, covering her white teeth with her hand in dismay.

'You'll love it,' Y.C. assured her, but she flatly refused to believe him.

After much discussion the food was chosen, and a troupe of petite oriental beauties in scarlet cheongsams appeared to distribute dishes of soy sauce and chillies. When tiny cups of fragrantly-scented Chinese tea had been poured out, Y.C. gave a lesson in how to handle chopsticks. This provoked much laughter, but as the meal progressed everyone managed a certain degree of skill. To the accompaniment of shrieks from the effervescent Terri they worked their way through eight courses before a final platter of fresh fruits—pineapple, orange slices, papaya and chunks of red water melon, was offered.

'I've eaten far too much.' Terri rubbed her stomach and pushed her plate away.

'But it was delicious,' Hogan said, smiling at Glenn. 'You certainly run a great hotel.'

The Australian beamed at the compliment and ordered up a round of liqueurs. The atmosphere was jovial, gradually the restaurant was becoming noisy with shouts of *'Yam Seng'*, a Chinese toast which surrounding tables were shouting out at the tops of their voices, holding on to the final note for as long as possible.

'There's your protégée,' Glenn whispered to Leah beneath the general hubub, and a drumroll sounded from the small group which had been providing background music. Everyone on their table turned to watch, but little reaction came from elsewhere. One or two people glanced over their shoulders, only to return to conversation or food.

'Jeez, wait for it,' Y.C. said, nervously smoothing down his black hair.

Leah did a double take when Jasmine stepped into the spotlight. Vaguely speaking the girl's dress could be termed a 'cheongsam', but it was *very* vaguely! The shimmering sheath of foxglove-pink sequins was tight fitting, with sidesplits which provided tantalising glimpses of smooth white thigh and a neckline which would have terrified a Las Vegas showgirl. Jasmine stepped forward and took a deep breath, nearly popping out of the keyhole cleavage, and began to sing a Cantonese lovesong in a reedy soprano. For the first few bars she remained motionless before the microphone, but gently her hips began to sway back and forth. Once having established a rhythm which owed nothing to the oriental music, the girl's undulations became more pronounced.

'The song might be olde worlde Cantonese, but the movements damn well aren't,' Glenn chuckled into Leah's ear.

Like a creature possessed, Jasmine began gyrating across the tiny dance floor, bumping and grinding, snaking out her legs, snapping her fingers and generally creating mayhem. Elbows began to nudge, chopsticks paused halfway to mouths, conversations faded. By now her song and the microphone had been forgotten, and Jasmine made no attempt to sing as dancing took control. The band, sensing all was not as rehearsed, switched tunes in midstream and swung into the latest Western disco hit. The Chinese girl really went to town.

'Get 'em off!' a voice shouted from the back of the room, and for one awful moment Leah wondered if her protégée might comply. She died a thousand deaths,

imagining Mr Tan's reaction when he discovered his
demure daughter had performed a striptease in one of
Hong Kong's leading hotels! She began to breathe again
when Jasmine wiggled a reproving finger and undulated
some more. Hands began clapping to the beat, there
were whistles and stamping which served as encourage-
ment, and the girl laughed, oozing and swaying to a
sensually impassioned finale. An encore was demanded,
which she energetically produced, and when the
performance came to an end Jasmine, with face flushed
and panting, received a standing ovation. She stood in
the spotlight blowing kisses until Y.C. went to her side.
Admirers crowded on to the dance floor to offer
enthusiastic praise, and several young men raised their
glasses.

'Perhaps that was not what had been planned, but
she sure as hell made an impact!' Glenn exclaimed,
grinning at all the fuss.

Leah struck the base of her hand against her brow in
despair. 'But what am I supposed to do now?' she
wailed.

'Grab a percentage,' Hogan said, and Leah flashed
him a hasty glance. Was he joking or not?

'Jasmine could have a great future,' the Australian
enthused.

'What as—a speciality dancer?' Hogan asked drily.
'She might go down a bomb here because it's Chinese
New Year and too much brandy has been poured down
too many throats, but basically she's no more than a
sexy female body and they're ten a penny.' He grinned
impudently across the table. 'Undress Leah and you'll
discover the same equipment.'

She paid him back with a look of fury. 'And what is
Mr Tan going to think?' she demanded. 'He's an old

fashioned, dyed-in-the-wool conservative. He'd have a fit if he suspected she was behaving like this!'

'Jasmine could have a great future,' Glenn declared once more.

'Well, if she does it will be with no help from me,' Leah retorted, redirecting her anger towards him. Couldn't he grasp that Jasmine was what Hogan had described and no more?

'You have a problem on your hands. Now that she's tasted glory she won't relish being the anonymous Miss Tan again,' Hogan pronounced, jerking his dark head towards the dance floor where Jasmine was lapping up the admiration.

When Glenn, forever the optimist, began praising the girl's talent again, Leah pushed back her chair. 'I'll go and get some fresh air. It's rather stuffy in here.'

'I'll come with you,' the Australian said, before she had time to resist.

As they travelled down in the lift, Leah realised that, like it or not, she had been given the perfect opportunity to tell Glenn how she felt about their relationship. It is now or never, she decided, steeling herself as he took her hand and led her out into the cool tranquillity of the dark gardens. But when he removed his dinner jacket and slipped it tenderly around her shoulders, murmuring that she must not get cold, her resolve began to crumble. How could she be ruthless when he was so kind, so pleasant, so loyal?

She took a deep breath. 'Er . . . I must be honest——' she began.

'Leah, for a long time——' he said at the same moment and they both laughed awkwardly. There was a taut silence, and then Glenn said, 'Suppose we get engaged at Easter?'

'But I don't love you!' she blurted out, her stomach twisting at his look of pain.

He pushed his hands deep into his trouser pockets, and gazed up at the moon. 'I guess that's us finished?' he sighed at last.

'I'm sorry, I should have made it plain long ago. I like you, Glenn, a lot, but . . .' Leah flung a distracted hand, knocking his jacket askew on her shoulders.

'Susie warned me,' he muttered.

'Susie?' She was too upset to follow his line of thought.

'Sue, disc jockey Sue.'

'Oh, I see,' she said, and subconsciously she registered that Sue would be happy to provide plenty of tender loving care if required.

'You're still in love with Hogan Whitney, aren't you?' he asked, but it sounded more like a statement than a question. 'I suppose I should have realised. You were worried sick about him yesterday evening.'

Leah's chin shot up. 'The only reason I was worried is because he represents a dollar-earner to Spencer Associates,' she retorted savagely.

'Hmm,' said the Australian.

They were carefully correct when they returned to the restaurant, smiling and talking like animated puppets. Jasmine had joined their table and was high on success. There was much laughter, lavish compliments were bandied around and more toasts drunk. Leah hoped the strain between herself and Glenn would pass unnoticed in the general high spirits, and decided no one was aware of their contretemps until she risked a glance at Hogan. In the brief instant when his grey eyes met hers she saw he was not fooled for his emotional antennae were too finely tuned in to hers. He danced with her once, in between dancing with Terri and Jasmine, but though he chatted pleasantly, making no reference to Glenn, she sensed his hidden awareness of the situation.

Midnight came and went, and tables around them were emptying.

'Time to call it a day,' Y.C. decided, taking Jasmine's arm.

'When can I have a second booking?' the Chinese girl giggled, glancing hopefully between Leah and Glenn.

Leah leapt in without giving the Australian a chance to speak. 'I'll be in touch in a week or two.'

Momentarily Jasmine looked disappointed, but she began to rally when Glenn praised her performance yet again.

'Use delaying tactics,' Y.C. whispered to Leah behind his hand. 'Tonight was great, but no way can she make this a habit. Old Man Tan would disinherit her if he knew!'

They shared a look of understanding, and Leah felt relieved that he was on her side. Prising Jasmine from the show business scene could be as tricky as prising a limpet from a rock.

Everyone trooped into the lift, Terri leaving at her floor and the others travelling down to the lobby. Glenn bade a hasty farewell and Y.C. steered Jasmine out towards the carpark.

'Violet is perpetually muttering about the cold, but for once I reckon she has a case,' Leah said, climbing ahead into the taxi Hogan had summoned with a flick of his fingers. She shivered, pulling her angora stole closer around her shoulders, for the night air was chill.

Hogan sat down beside her and lifted an arm. 'I'll keep you warm,' he offered and when she looked doubtful, he grinned. 'Relax, kitten. Furtive gropings in the back of taxis are not my style.'

'Oh no!' she said archly, remembering moments from the past.

'Well, not tonight,' he qualified, so half against her better judgment and because she was cold, she nestled into the curve of his arm.

'Do you think Terri *does* report back to Saul, in general, I mean?' she mused, as the taxi sped along through the darkness. She was beginning to feel warmer now, comforted by Hogan's body heat. He felt so firm, so familiar as he held her close.

'It's hard to tell. She gives the impression of being straight, and from odd things she's let slip I gather her reaction to her dear uncle is much the same as ours, but I never underestimate Saul. He's probably bugged one of those shiny white teeth without her knowing!' He ran his fingers reflectively across his dark moustache. 'Why do you ask?'

'I was wondering if he's likely to hear about Jasmine's success this evening, and I would much rather he don't. Saul has few scruples and if there is a whiff of money around, he'll be interested.'

'That's true! For five dollars he'd offload his grandmother to white slave traders,' Hogan said drily. 'But I didn't imagine Jasmine will make much money. She's more likely to wind up parading semiclad in some sleazy nightclub.'

Leah shivered again, but not from the cold. 'Then I really ought to nip her career in the bud.'

'Does it ever strike you that perhaps you and your illustrious boss have more in common than you would care to admit?' he enquired, and there was a stony edge to his voice. 'You have the power to make or break

Jasmine, and you have just decided to break.'

'But it's what is best for her!' she retorted, hurt by the unfairness of his accusation.

'In this case I agree, but do you never stop to think that the way Saul plays the public relations game it resembles moving pawns around on a board, and those pawns are people!'

'Like you?' she demanded, pulling back from him.

'No, I'm not in any danger, I can look after myself and I do. I'm perfectly capable of playing Saul at his own game,' he said calmly. 'But I've watched him in action with less dominant souls, and I know he'll use every trick in the book if necessary.'

'You forget that I am not Saul!' Her words cut like knives. 'Most of my work entails promoting products or company images, not individuals.'

Hogan raised a sardonic brow. 'So far maybe, but what happens if you go . . . *when* you go higher up the scale?'

'I don't know if I am going any higher with Spencer Associates,' she began, but the taxi came to a stop outside the entrance to the apartments, and there was the diversion of the exchange of dollars and good-nights.

Hogan picked up the thread of conversation as the lift moved upwards. 'You'll reach the top in Spencer Associates unless you opt out of being a career girl and marry, but that seems unlikely.'

'You reckon I'm a confirmed spinster?' she demanded.

His grey eyes scraped over her. 'Yes, I do,' he said, with deliberate insolence. 'What the hell do you want from a man, Leah? You turned me down and this evening you sent Glenn packing. He seems a reliable type, perfect family man, I imagine.'

'What happened between Glenn and me is private, it's nothing to do with you.' She stalked out of the lift and made for her apartment.

'It has everything to do with me,' he growled, striding along beside her. Hogan's sword might be in its scabbard, but the flash of steel showed. 'You led that poor bastard up the garden path! I feel so sorry for him because I know exactly what he's going through right now. Don't forget I've been there myself.'

Leah pivoted to him. 'Don't rewrite history, Hogan. I never turned you down for the simple reason you never asked me to marry you.' She stabbed her key into the lock and flung wide the door. 'Goodnight!'

'Oh yes, I did.' His voice was soft but firm.

She wheeled round. 'Daydreams about sharing a cottage in the South of France don't constitute a proposal, nor do hazy plans for a future together!'

'No, I agree. But you had it in black and white, what more did you want?'

She pushed a weary hand into the thick flaxen hair at her temple. 'You've had a busy day, Hogan, we both have, and you're not making sense. Let's just forget it, shall we?'

'No, we damn well won't.' His voice vibrated, sounding too loud in the marble-walled corridor. 'That's always been the trouble with us, we never did get down to talking. But I want to talk, and talk now! I need to know what the hell went wrong and why you never even had the courtesy to answer my letter.'

'I don't remember any letter,' she said scathingly, wondering obliquely if this was some ploy to get her alone in the dead of the night when her defences were down. They were not only down, they were damn near nonexistent! Sitting beside him in the taxi she had had to resist the urge to rest her head on his broad shoulder and cuddle closer. Her fingers had ached to reach out and trace the line of his lips beneath the bristly moustache.

'Then you have a short memory, Miss Morrison,' he barked and reached past her to flick on the wall-lights in the living-room.

'We can talk tomorrow,' she said, but her voice was uncertain. The mention of a letter was intriguing.

He gripped her shoulder and steered her inside. 'We talk *now*,' he ground out. 'And for starters you can explain why you didn't have the decency to reply with a simple "no".' He glared at her as she moved around like an automaton, drawing the heavy brocade curtains and turning on twin bars of the log fire. 'Have you any idea of the torment I went through?'

Leah rounded on him, hands at her hips. 'Some torment!' she sneered. 'When you were busy speeding around the highways and byways with that Brazilian bombshell.'

'Get your facts straight.' Hogan held aloft an imperious index finger. 'One—the girl happened to be the daughter of a Brazilian motor manufacturer who sponsors me. When I had visited Brazil I had been entertained in great style, so it seemed a civilised gesture to return their hospitality. If you hadn't been off on one of your career jaunts we would have made up a threesome. As it was, I showed her the sights.'

'Your etchings?' she said waspishly.

Scowling, he raised a second finger. 'Two—she was a pleasant girl and I liked her, but that was all. There was no affair. Don't forget I was madly in love with you, *then*.'

Leah didn't know what to say or where to look.

Somewhere, hidden in the secret places of her mind, she had hoped Hogan might still care, but the tiny bud which had unreasonably blossomed was now ground underfoot. *Then*, he had said, setting his love firmly in the past.

'Three—I was waiting for you to return, when fate decided otherwise. The accident cancelled out Wimbledon and you never came back.' His hand fell to his side. 'There was ample time to think in hospital, and as soon as I was fit enough to be propped up in bed I wrote. I asked you to marry me.'

Leah was muddled. 'Something isn't right here,' she frowned, thinking aloud. 'I never received your letter.'

'But Saul sent . . .' His voice trailed off as their eyes met in mutual comprehension. The connection of Saul's involvement in the flowers Leah had sent, and now the letter, was too much. Hogan flopped down on to the sofa, swearing beneath his breath. 'The interfering bastard!'

'Would you like a drink?' asked Leah as she struggled to make sense of the situation.

'Good idea, a brandy please, and then I'll tell you my side of the story.' He waited until she sat down beside him then hesitated, staring down into his goblet as he thoughtfully swirled the amber-brown liquid. 'I suppose it all hinges on my crash. When my leg was mangled everyone rushed around offering kind words and sympathy, yet deep down every man jack of them believed I was finished.' He shook his head, pushing back the thick hair from his brow in weary disbelief. 'There was this unreal air of vitality. My father gave pep talks on how I'd soon be running around again, my mother brought in ghastly books about cripples who'd made it to the South Pole and back, tennis colleagues breezed in and out talking heartily of the matches we would play in the future. Yet basically they knew, and I knew, that it was drivel! I reached an all-time low. I felt I was a physical and mental wreck, no good for anything. I was grovelling on rock-bottom when Saul appeared. He was so damn positive, he was convinced I *did* have a future.' Hogan threw a glance at the sceptical tilt of her head. 'Maybe it was Saul's usual bull in a china shop approach or maybe he had good timing. Maybe I would have pulled out of the depression on my own, I don't know. What I do know is that when he bellowed that I should get the hell out of bed and back on to the tennis courts where I belonged, I felt a tremendous surge of relief and energy. Life was a viable proposition again, thanks to Saul.'

'So he persuaded you to start back?'

Hogan took a slug of brandy. 'Yes. I know he's a devious bastard, but I owe him for that.'

Leah was beginning to understand. 'Which is why you have stayed with Spencer Associates although you're unhappy about his ethics?'

He nodded. 'In my cynical moments I now suspect he wanted me on the move because he could see that my recovery made a great sob story, and there was a healthy profit to be gained from that angle.' Hogan lifted a shoulder into a dismissive shrug. 'Whatever his motives, he provided the right stimulus at the right time. He made me realise there was a light at the end of the tunnel. He bullied me on to a walking frame, had me exercising in the pool, all that jazz. When the sponsors hinted they might want to cut loose, he persuaded them to hang on. He appeared to have my interests at heart, yet he must have deliberately held back the letter to you which I asked him to forward.'

She frowned. 'But why didn't you telephone or write again when there was no reply?'

'Because I had had second thoughts. I told you I had had time to think, perhaps I had too much time. Don't forget that you had never bothered to get in touch,' he growled, unable to keep the bitterness from his voice.

'But I *did!* I sent two dozen red roses and a note saying . . . saying I cared. I told you I'd fly home the minute you asked me.'

'I remember the roses, but there was no note, no indication of who had sent them. When I asked Saul, he said they had been left by an unknown admirer.' His lips jammed together beneath the thick moustache. 'God, I could kill him!'

'He was protecting his investment,' Leah said in a flat voice. 'You must realise that you are far more marketable as a glamour boy. Any attachments would spoil the image.' There was a mixture of scorn and misery in her voice. 'And the image is tailor-made.'

'Is that what you believe?' he challenged.

She tossed her hair back from her shoulder. 'What I believe is immaterial.'

Hogan caught hold of her fingers, interlacing them with his own. 'No, it's not, kitten.'

'Why don't you leave Saul and let some other public relations firm deal with your affairs? Even if you do owe him for setting you back on the road to recovery, you're not in his debt for ever.' She was gazing down at their hands. His was large and masculine, strong tanned fingers with the nails cut short and straight. Her hand was pale and tapered, with rose lacquered nails.

He narrowed his eyes. 'Whose side are you on? Don't forget I indirectly contribute to your salary and keep you installed in that fancy office.'

'That's not important,' she cried. 'Be realistic.'

'I am. I know damn well that should I fail to deliver Saul will cut and run, having made certain every last drop of lucrative juice has been squeezed from me.'

'Well then!'

'But don't forget that right now he's squeezing out the money on my behalf. Saul works *for me*, not the other way round, never forget that!' he insisted. 'As a publicist he's a shrewd operator. He might be a shark, but that's life. He's one of the best in the business, and unfortunately if I changed companies Saul might angle the break so that everyone would wonder what was wrong with me, not him. I can't afford that now, not as things are.' Hogan glanced at her astutely as though wondering whether he had said too much, and swiftly reangled the conversation. 'So you reckon he deliberately demolished our love affair?'

'In truth there wasn't much demolishing to do, was there? He merely kicked aside the rubble,' she replied, with a flippancy she was far from feeling.

'I would have said we had foundations, rather than rubble. Okay, so the last few weeks before Wimbledon had been . . .' Hogan paused, searching painfully for the right word. 'Tricky, but——'

'It was the beginning of the end,' Leah cut in remorselessly. 'Our affair had already burned itself out, the firework display was over.'

'You're wrong, the Catherine wheels are still spinning for us, kitten.' His grey eyes slid over her, making promises. 'This morning we proved we light up the skies together.'

He took her empty goblet from her fingers, setting it aside and only pausing to ease open the buttons of his black dinner jacket before he slid a strong arm around her waist, dragging her against him. Rockets exploded piecemeal in Leah's head as he bent, inflaming her throat and the sensitive hollow beneath her ear with lingering kisses. His breath, smelling faintly of brandy, seared along her skin.

'No, Hogan.' She pushed at his shirt front, but he took no notice, merely raising the protesting fingers to his lips and kissing them one by one. His mouth moved to her palm, his tongue circling and tasting in an erotic declaration of intent which made Leah's veins sparkle with golden rain. 'No,' she heard herself mutter, but the protest was fragile, and when his mouth covered hers, hard and possessive, she found her arms twisting around his neck and her body tilting to arch against him.

'Do you know the effect you're having on me?' he complained, but she could hear satisfaction in his voice.

As the langourous domination of his mouth continued, she discovered exactly the effect she was having, for Hogan's breathing quickened and his hard muscles throbbed his desire. Yet his movements were unhurried, he was taking his time, reading the message from the lips clinging to his and the female form pliant beneath him, as one of unconditional surrender. Gently he edged the soft chiffon from her shoulders, nuzzling with tender love bites until Leah sighed, revisiting a dream. His grey eyes darkened with passion as they feasted on the creamy globes of her breasts with their honeyed pinnacles.

'You're so beautiful,' he murmured as his tanned fingers stroked the incredible smoothness, caught at the silky nipples until she was forced to whimper. His dark head moved down, his mouth opening on to the swollen curves, his lips teasing and tantalising the rigid nubs into such sensitivity that Leah began tugging at his shirt, desperate for the sensation of his flesh against hers. Hogan raised himself to pull the buttons free, tossing both his jacket and shirt aside.

'I swear no one else has ever made me feel . . .' His purring baritone faded as he devoted himself to her again.

The Catherine wheel juddered. Female bodies were ten a penny, he had said. Leah's spinning senses began to steady and she pressed against his shoulders, trying to bring an end to his kisses. 'It's late, you must go,' she implored, instinctively knowing that if she did not forestall his lovemaking she would be trapped, hopelessly in his spell—like so many other women . . .

With the tip of his finger Hogan traced a circle around the rigid peak of her breast, making her bite down hard to quench a gasp of desire. He had always known how to arouse her.

'Let's make love, that's what we both need,' he murmured, his voice low and aching. 'Kitten, you're ready. We're both ready.'

Another conversation from the past swirled into her head—how Saul had suggested Hogan have a few affairs in order to relieve his tension, and how *she* had been firmly placed in that category. With abrupt violence, she fought free, jolting from his arms as she gathered the crumpled chiffon around her. 'Making love doesn't fall within my duties,' she said, and was dismayed when a sob broke into her words. 'Running round in circles after you might, but relieving your tension does not.'

Hogan looked at her, then gulped in a deep breath as he regained a measure of control. 'Leah, any relief from tension would be mutual.'

Eyes flashing like green icicles, she glared at him. 'I can't have made myself clear at the outset. My remit as the local representative of Spencer Associates does not cover *all* your whims!'

She had been about to say more, but Hogan's swift rise to his feet made the words catch in her throat. With nostrils flared, he towered above her, his passion now directed into a white-hot anger.

'I keep forgetting that I have no clear knowledge of just how much you live in Saul's pocket,' he sneered. 'What is your remit? Keep me happy, but never forget the almighty dollar? Do everything you can for me so long as it brings in cold hard cash but if it doesn't then don't bother?' He reached down and picked up his dinner jacket, sliding a hand into the inner pocket. With deadly deliberation he removed a leather wallet and began thumbing off notes, switching his eyes between Leah and the money in a calculated insult. 'Long haired blondes can't come cheap, but everything has its price. Your beloved boss will have taught you that.'

'Get out,' she screamed, as he held out a wad of notes. 'Get out!'

Hogan gave a taunting bow. 'With the greatest of pleasure.'

CHAPTER SIX

AFTER a restless night, morning saw Leah's grim mood ripening into an uncharacteristic need for revenge. She had little choice other than to continue supervising Hogan's promotional activities, but that supervision would be kept to a bare minimum. If he insisted he pay for her favours then he could start by paying for her smiles! And the minute the business part of his trip came to an end, he was on his own. She was determined not to lift so much as a finger on his behalf during his holiday week. So what if he was landed in a strange apartment, in a strange city, in a strange country, that was his lookout! Her blood boiled when she considered his sneering attack. To link her with the money-grubbing Saul had been blatantly unfair, and Hogan knew it! In typically male fashion, he had tilted the scales in his favour for not only had he depicted her as a calculating monster, he had also inferred he had been a blameless victim, jilted virtually on his deathbed.

The truth was a different matter. By his own admission he had been at rock-bottom when he had decided to write and ask her to marry him. Hogan had been clutching at straws, but it was remarkable how, the minute his confidence returned, he had realised that straws were only straws. Straws blew away in the wind. Straws were chewed and spat out.

This morning a blanket of sodden grey cloud smothered Hong Kong, greasing the pavements, smearing against the windows, blurring the islands, the ocean, the jagged peaks. With the damp had come cold, and even Leah felt chilly enough to wear a cosy black sweater and matching cords, adding an embroidered black velvet matador jacket for good measure. Today she plaited back her hair into a gleaming flaxen twist at the nape of her neck and applied a touch of blusher to cover the paleness of her cheeks, before concentrating on her eyes. She used a pearly-grey shadow, in keeping with the weather and her mood, adding a delicate line of kohl and lashings of sooty mascara. Her lips were outlined in deep rose, their soft fullness coloured in a paler shade. Now she could face the world and, regrettably, Hogan.

Today his programme was less hectic. The first appointment was his luncheon talk at Mr Tan's golf club, and that promised to be a relaxed and informal occasion. At least something was relaxed! Leah's nerves, zinging taut with resentment over Hogan's attack, meant *she* was liable to screech out loud at the slightest provocation. She forced herself to check through his schedule. She must make sure he was delivered to the television studios in good time for the chat show early evening. Leah made a note to ask when he wanted to rearrange his postponed interview with the lady journalist. After a cup of coffee, for she was in no mood to eat, she tugged on high-heeled black leather boots, yanking up the zips with a decisiveness that was still apparent in the tense line of her jaw when she knocked at Hogan's door.

'Ready?' she demanded, daring him to say he wasn't.

'Just.' He was wearing his brown leather jacket over a cream silk shirt and slacks. He was freshly shaved and neat, his thick dark hair brushed smoothly back over his ears.

'Let's go.'

The hostility was barely muted. Whatever friendship had existed before had now been destroyed and when Leah noticed he displayed the faintest of limps, she decided he deserved no sympathy whatsoever. It was mid-morning, if he had wished to exercise his leg back into mobility, he had had ample time.

'Has Terri been over for a physio session?' she enquired sweetly, making a great show of frowning at the way he was walking.

He slashed a sour glance. 'You know damn well she hasn't! Perhaps I should have got up earlier, but I was tired. You said we have a long journey out to the golf club this morning, so there'll be plenty of time in the taxi for me to flex the muscles.'

'We're not taking a taxi. Roger left his car and as the club is way out in the New Territories I thought I might as well drive us out there myself.' When they reached the basement car park Leah marched out of the lift. 'This is it,' she said, unlocking the door of a battered little runabout which appeared to be held together by sticky tape and not much else. She caught Hogan's look of horror. 'It might not be as flash as your Porsche back home, but it'll get us there.'

'And back?' he enquired laconically.

Ignoring him, Leah slid into the driving seat. 'Get in,' she said, reaching across to open the passenger door.

'No!' Hogan was resolute, his lips a straight line beneath the bristles of his moustache. 'There isn't enough room. How the hell am I supposed to work on my leg if I'm trapped in a glorified egg-box?'

Leah was furious. He was sabotaging her arrangements yet again.

'Talk about prima donna tactics!' She jumped out of

the car, nearly spitting in her anger. 'All this adulation has gone to your head, Hogan. Okay so you're a glamour boy, so big deal! You might be everybody else's idol but you're damn well not mine. In my book you're only a man who hits balls over nets and you've been nothing but one great big headache ever since you arrived.' She slammed shut the car door with such violence that flakes of rust showered the ground. 'Come on. I'll go and see if I can rustle up a limousine if that suits your requirements, *sir!*'

She was glaring at him as though she had long known he was the type to kick a man, and women and children too, when they were down. All thumbs and fiery mutterings, Leah fumbled with the keys attempting to lock the door and stalk away, but Hogan gave a hoot of laughter.

'Oh kitten,' he crowed, slapping the roof of the car in his delight. 'Do you know, that's the first time in ages anyone has dared to say what they think? Usually it's "yes Hogan, no Hogan". Even if I make people livid they keep the smiles glued on. And you don't have to provide a limousine, I'm quite happy to travel in this heap of junk so long as I can sit in the back.' He bent to peer into the rear window. 'I can stretch out my leg on the seat and wiggle my toes.'

Leah was deflated, but she also felt much better after her outburst. When she drove the little car up the basement ramp and out into the city streets, a watery sun was lurking behind the clouds and the morning did not seem too unbearable after all.

'Happy now?' Hogan teased, and she allowed him half a smile through the driving mirror. He was propped up on the back seat like some invalid potentate.

'You seldom find chauffeurs driving two-bit bone-shakers like this,' she commented, screwing up her face as she made a difficult change into second gear. 'I'll apologise for the fits and starts in advance. The car hasn't been used since Roger went on leave and it always did have a mind of its own.'

At length the concrete jungle petered out, the pressures of driving in heavy traffic slackened and Leah began to feel more at ease with the car, with herself, and with Hogan. The New Territories were less densely populated, and she always enjoyed escaping for a while from the hurly-burly, from the crowded streets between the high buildings, from the incessant noise. Although they passed through one or two towns, there were long stretches of quiet road where grassy hillsides replaced skyscrapers and there were farms instead of acres of real estate. The sun broke through as they left the coast, little scraps of blue showing amidst the white lace of the clouds.

Hogan was fascinated by the place names—Sheung Kwai Chung, Kwun Yam Keng, Hong Ha Po; by the washing which dripped from bamboo poles, and by the people. The pseudo-Western world of central Hong Kong had been left behind. Now black-pyjamaed old ladies, half hidden beneath coolie hats with deep black frills, trudged along the roadside. Sloe-eyed children scampered around ponds herding flocks of poultry this way and that. Labourers wielded obscure farming tackle in the fields. As they motored along, they chatted easily and Leah was pleased to share her limited knowledge of the Colony. Finally Hogan grew silent and when Leah cast a quick glance through the mirror, she discovered he was lying with his eyes closed. He seemed peaceful, but when she spotted the tell-tale nerve leaping in his temple she felt chastened. Perhaps she should have ordered a comfortable limousine. He had obviously underplayed the problem with the leg muscle and considering the matter, Leah began to feel anxious.

They passed through a village, travelling out again into peaceful green countryside, and she had time to study him, her white teeth tugging uneasily at her lower lip. She was so engrossed that when a toddler appeared ahead, wafting several ducks into the path of the car, the obstruction took her by surprise. Leah jammed on the brakes. The little car skidded, bodywork complaining madly, the toddler leapt aside, and there was a soft thud and a frantic quacking. Hogan shot forward, slamming against the back of the seats as he groped wildly, arms and legs flying.

'Bloody hell! What are you doing?' he demanded, his voice harsh with pain. Wincing, he pushed himself back on to the seat, protecting his thigh with both hands. 'You know I must avoid any knocks and here you are, flinging me around like a rag doll!'

Heart racing, Leah switched off the engine. 'I had to brake, there was no other option. I'm sorry.' Her tone, to conceal a giddying sense of disaster, was reasonable.

'I should damn well think you are!'

'Are you okay?' she asked, her voice cracking.

He muttered something vicious beneath his breath and continued holding his thigh.

She didn't know what to do. The child, she couldn't tell from its pyjama suit whether it was a boy or girl, stood at the side of the road sucking a thumb and staring at them. The shrill quacking continued and when a duck landed on the bonnet, its webbed feet slapping obscenely, Leah flinched. Her nerves were in shreds. 'Hogan,' she said in a choked voice. 'I think I may have killed something.'

'Stay here. I'll take a look,' he ordered and hobbled out.

She sat like stone, hands gripping the wheel so tightly that her fingers turned white. She could imagine a duck, or perhaps two, mangled beneath the car, still half alive, quacking piteously, blood and entrails spilling out on to the road. Oh God! what would Hogan do, kill them with his bare hands to put them out of their misery? Instead he flapped his arms so that the duck on the bonnet gave a squawk and departed, then jerked his thumb at the child on the verge. The child stared at him. He came to Leah's window.

'How do you say "beat it" in Chinese? There's no fatality, just enough loose feathers to fill a mattress.' He nodded towards the ducks, now waddling around the child. 'That lot needn't worry, they'll still make it to the dinner table."

'Lucky ducks,' she managed to say, her voice hovering between laughter and tears.

Hogan went round the car, flexing his leg as he walked, and eased himself into the front seat beside her. 'Kitten, don't be upset. No harm's done.' He touched her cheek with his fingertips, smiling gently into the green eyes which were bright with unshed tears. 'It was an accident and who knows better than me about how easily accidents can happen?'

'Oh Hogan,' she gasped, and suddenly she was sobbing against his chest.

'There, there. Everything is all right,' he assured her, holding her close as he stroked her hair and kissed her brow.

Leah leant against him, soaking up his strength, his

calm. 'I thought I'd killed a duck and I knew I'd hurt you,' she gulped, searching in her bag for tissues. She dabbed at her wet cheeks. 'Are you sure there's no damage to your leg?'

'It's fine,' he soothed, waiting as she regained her composure.

With a final sniff, Leah pushed the tissues away and looked at her watch. 'We're not in any rush, so I'll go a little slower from now on. Do you want to sit in the back?'

'No thanks, I reckon I'm safer posted here as lookout.' He grinned to show he was teasing. 'As I said before, once I get moving the leg's fine. I won't have any more trouble with it today.'

Leah turned the key in the ignition. 'I don't believe you,' she said, concentrating on the road. She motored up through the gears and when they were once more driving peacefully along, she continued, 'Tell me the truth, are you going to be able to break back into professional tennis with a handicap like that?'

She had deliberately chosen the word 'handicap', expecting him to react strongly, but instead Hogan gave an outward breath of despair.

'I don't know.'

'Is the condition of your leg deteriorating?'

The muscles of his neck tightened involuntarily. 'Yes.'

'So if you continue non-stop exercising, and running, and all the tennis aren't you in danger of doing irreversible damage?'

'Possibly.' He thought for a moment. 'No, *probably!*' he snarled, but his anger was not directed at her. Hogan ran both hands through his hair, dragging it back from his temples. 'When I first restarted my training schedule the muscle was tense and occasionally my leg seized up, but the spasm was brief. About a month ago I noticed that instead of only stiffness first thing in the morning, there was a weakness, too. I lied to you. I have fallen over before.' With every sentence he seemed to be lifting mountains. 'Now I require half an hour's exercise before the muscle is strong enough to support me completely.'

'Shouldn't you go back and discuss the problem with your surgeon?' she asked.

He swore beneath his breath. 'No, because I know damn fine what he'll say.'

Leah sighed. 'No tennis.'

Her phrase, like a stone thrown into a pool, caused endless thought ripples and they drove along in silence, each considering the matter.

'How can I opt out now?' Hogan asked at length. 'There are millions of dollars invested in me. Besides,' he added quickly, my leg *might* be strong enough to allow me to make a reasonable bid for a few titles. It's not as though my tennis has suffered much yet.'

'What about the other evening?' she asked, keeping her voice neutral.

'I was tired.'

'Only tired?' she prodded. 'Everyone else seemed to imagine you were deliberately forcing a cliff-hanger, but you weren't, were you, Hogan? I've seen you play when you've been tired but you never played in such a cramped style before. You were lucky the match took place in Hong Kong. If you had played like that in Europe or America there would have been some pretty searching questions.'

He gave her a thundery glare. 'I won! If I pace myself I'll be okay. I still have the tenacity to win.'

'You have the tenacity to ruin that leg for ever,' she snapped, swinging on to the granite-chipped drive towards the golf club. 'Why are you doing this? You have the nerve to infer my motivation is money, but you're putting wealth before your health, and that doesn't make much sense!'

'Forgive me for last night,' he said heavily. 'You made me hopping mad so I needed to be cruel, but I lied. I'm all chewed up about my leg at the moment and I tend to fly off the handle and say things I don't mean.'

'Apology accepted,' she said in a tart tone which indicated that though she might forgive, she wasn't prepared to forget. 'Face it, Hogan, you deride Saul because he worships money, but at least he isn't prepared to *cripple* himself for it!'

'I don't give a damn about the cash. I have enough already.'

'So you're frightened of upsetting your sponsors!' she taunted with fruity disbelief. 'But we all know how sponsors jump on and off gravy trains at every other station. I'm sure your legal advisers could come up with a reasonable settlement to keep them happy.'

Hogan stared out at the rolling greens of the golf course without seeing a thing. 'Okay, okay, the sponsors could be paid off, but what about me?' he demanded, striking an open hand against his chest. Leah realised she had forced him to admit the truth of his dilemma. 'The life of a tennis player is all I know. Since I left school a clutch of rackets has been my only baggage, my passport to success, to satisfaction. Tennis has been the mainspring of my life!'

Bringing the little car to a halt beneath the portico of the clubhouse, Leah switched off the engine and turned to him.

'I doubt any one else in the whole wide world knows that better than I,' she said coldly and climbed out to greet Mr Tan.

The golf club luncheon proved to be a great success. Hogan displayed his usual charm, talking with the locals who clustered at his elbow and later entertaining them with a humorous and interesting description of his life in the higher echelons of tennis. Leah found it difficult to believe that there was a man who had reached a vital crossroads in his life. But image is everything, she thought wryly, and where would Hogan be without tennis? More to the point, *what* would Hogan be without tennis?

Afterwards Mr Tan insisted on a tour of the golf course with club officials and most of the men clambered into a fleet of small buggies and phut-phutted away. Leah had been hoping for a few quiet moments in their absence, but found herself buttonholed by two local businessmen, one in banking and the other a herbalist, who quoted Mr Tan's glowing reports on her expertise. They were keen to hear her suggestions as to how Spencer Associates might help them, and she made an appointment to meet up with the banker for a further discussion, but kept the herbalist at bay.

'To be honest my knowledge of your trade is minimal. I know nothing about cures of crushed deer antlers or snake gall,' she stalled, feeling very much the Westerner.

'And ginseng,' he added, nodding enthusiastically. 'Next week I send you samples. You try them.'

She forced a grateful smile. 'That's very kind. I'll come back to you if I can work up some ideas,' she promised, sidling away.

Hogan returned from the inspection of the course with several golf dates arranged and they took their leave, Leah aware of how disreputable Roger's car really was when everyone piled out of the clubhouse to watch them drive off.

'You have made a great hit with Mr Tan,' Hogan commented. 'All the way round to the eighteenth hole he was regaling me with your flair.'

She smiled, then asked anxiously, 'Did he mention Jasmine's cabaret spot?'

'He said he had heard she received plenty of applause,' Hogan chuckled. 'But he's under the impression it was for her singing! However, he did seem anxious about whether her career would prove to be a good investment in the long term because apparently her star-spangled outfit cost the earth and the return from the Dynasty was peanuts. Now Madam Jasmine expects her daddy to fork out on a second expensive dress.'

Leah grinned. 'But Mr Tan, with his abacus of a mind, is beginning to wonder if Jasmine's career is quite so vital, after all,' she deduced.

'His face did fall when I pointed out that if his daughter intends to spread her wings there'll be more outfits to be financed, and hairdresser's bills, and air fares, and hotel charges, and taxis, and——'

'And Spencer Associates percentage,' she piped up.

Hogan gave her an old-fashioned look. 'Said like a trouper.'

She noticed a slight drop in temperature. 'Thanks for doing some groundwork on my behalf,' she smiled, wanting to restore the previous lighthearted camaraderie. Jibes about her career she could do without.

'When I play golf with Mr Tan I'll drop out a few

more disadvantages, financial and otherwise,' he assured her.

'I'd appreciate that.' Now they appeared to be back on course again. 'How would you feel about modelling some of his casual wear?' she asked. 'On a one-off basis?'

'Ye gods, you never miss a trick, do you?' he groaned, but he was laughing.

'The Fast-Lane range includes cagoules, flying jackets and sweatshirts. All macho stuff,' Leah said, determined to soldier on.

'I wouldn't have to wear make-up, would I?' asked Hogan cautiously. 'I can't stand having that muck on my face.'

She arched a brow. 'You surprise me. I would have thought prune eyeshadow and a touch of terracotta blusher would have been just your style.' Hogan chuckled. 'Plus a handbag to carry on that limp wrist of yours.'

'There's nothing limp about me,' he protested, and grabbed hold of the hand she had moved to the gear stick. 'Here, feel.'

Laughing, Leah pulled free. 'I believe you! Now, leave me alone. It's dangerous to interfere with the driver.'

'Dangerous, but fun,' he drawled. 'And that's a specific, not a generalisation.'

The television interview turned out to be the same old routine. What is life like behind the sport? Tell us about the training and the tension. Reveal any spicy incidents in the locker room. How does it feel to have a metal leg? And what of the future? Hogan fielded this last one gracefully.

Knuckles folded beneath her chin, Leah sat in the dark anonymity of the audience and studied him. For the past decade he had spent forty weeks a year on the globe-trotting hothouse tennis circuit. Most of his happiest moments had come from tennis, and his worst. He had coped with the bitter rivalries, the dramas, the superstitions, the venom. The intense orgy of happiness when he had been victorious, and the dull thud of defeat. He had been immersed in the self-obsessed tennis world for the major part of his life and yet, amazingly, he was able to converse articulately and interestingly about a wide range of other topics, given the chance. He was no one-dimensional zombie like so many other tennis aces she had met. Hogan was an enthusiastic member of the human race. Leah's creative imagination leapt into overdrive...

'Would you like to come and have a drink?' she asked when they returned to the apartments later that evening.

He cast her a wary glance. 'What do you have lined up? If it's another "I blow hot, I blow cold" session, I'll pass.'

She refused to rise to his bait. 'I've been considering your dilemma and I would like to offer a few observations, for what they're worth.'

'Are you still wearing your Spencer Associates hat?' he demanded, reluctant to be persuaded.

'This has nothing to do with business,' she assured him as she unlocked the door. 'Contrary to your accusation, I don't consider myself to be Saul's puppet. I treat him with caution, much the same as you, but obviously as he's my boss I am under his jurisdiction to a certain degree.'

Hogan subjected her to a long level look. 'I've

already apologised for my outburst. I have a quick temper, and everything I said was in the heat of the moment. I know fine that where it matters you function independently.' He gave a twisted grin. 'Believe me, I would never have been frank about my leg problem if I had ever really imagined you would report back.'

'So we know where we stand? Good,' she smiled when he nodded.

Hogan followed her into the apartment. 'Do you think you could make that drink into a coffee, and is there anything to eat? Those vol-au-vent things they handed round at the television studios were so damn small. I gobbled down six in quick succession, but then I had the feeling the producer was keeping count, so . . .'

'How about bacon and eggs?' she asked. 'And if you're still a yoghurt fiend I have some bizarre oriental varieties in stock.'

He grinned at her. 'Sounds great.'

As Leah grilled the bacon and prepared the eggs, Hogan set out cups and saucers on the small pine breakfast-bar in the corner of the kitchen.

'I have a curious feeling of *déjà vu*, kitten,' he said, coming behind her as she stood at the cooker. He slid his arms around her waist, brushing his face against her hair. 'We had some wonderful evenings together in your London flat. The only trouble was that there weren't enough of them.' He bent his head to kiss the nape of her neck, his mouth warm and avid. 'You'd prepare supper and afterwards we'd sit in the glow of the fire and listen to records. We'd make a little love and later have a bath together, and go to bed. God!' he said, pressing closer against her so that she could feel the hard length of his body. 'It was so *good*.'

She took a deep breath, moving determinedly away

on the pretext of checking the eggs. 'But it was mainly physical,' she said coolly. 'Relationships need more, at least for me they do,' she added, recalling Hogan's on-off love affairs. 'Because the sexual side was so ... so pyrotechnic, we imagined we were in love, but we weren't. It was a sham.' She was using 'we', but really she meant 'you'. Her love had been real, it was Hogan's that had been fake. She swivelled to face him, the grilling tongs in her hand. 'Let's learn from our mistakes and keep things simple between us from now on.' She sliced the tongs through the air. 'I want our relationship to be platonic, Hogan. No more kissing and touching. Let's just be good friends.' If they played with fire someone would be burned, and Leah knew she could not stand the pain.

His eyes met and held hers for a long enquiring moment. 'If that's what you really want,' he began uncertainly. 'But——'

'No buts. You're only here for a short time, so——'

'So I'd better keep my hands to myself and have a look in the fridge at your bizarre oriental yoghurt?' he quipped, but she could tell he was hurt.

Yet was he hurt, or merely offended? Leah did not know. By insisting they keep their relationship platonic she had winded his ego, that was all. Probably Hogan's idea of himself as an irresistible powerhouse of physical attraction had been knocked off balance, but he soon seemed to recover. By the time the bacon and eggs had been eaten they were both relaxed again and, try as she might, Leah failed to detect any hidden undercurrents in their conversation.

'Mangosteen yoghurt!' he quoted, raising his eyebrows as he ripped the lid from the tub with more energy than expertise. The foil tore and he ended up sucking yoghurt from his fingers. 'It's good,' he said, with a grin.

'Here,' Leah leant across the table to dab at his face with her napkin. 'You're covered in the stuff.'

He caught hold of her wrist. 'Why don't you lick it off my moustache for me?' he teased, eyes glinting.

'Sometimes you can be as aggravating as hell,' she snapped, struggling to free her hand as a turmoil of desire and despair wrestled within her. When Hogan let go she placed two hands flat on the table and glared at him. 'We'd agreed that from now on everything is to be platonic.'

He blew her an irreverent kiss. 'You know how it is between us, kitten. Do you honestly believe——'

'Yes, I do,' she bit out. Galvanised into action by the fear that if she didn't do something, Hogan would, she began frantically clearing away the dishes.

'I apologise,' he said at length, spooning out the last of the creamy yoghurt and watching with unconcealed amusement as she reeled around the tiny kitchen like a dancing dervish. He adopted a look of saintly innocence. 'I'll be a good little boy.'

'You'd better,' she warned him. 'And I mean it. I shall send you packing if you don't behave yourself.'

'Yes, ma'am,' he said, properly meek.

He helped her with the washing-up, keeping the conversation to generalities, apparently now determined not to upset her equilibrium. When the kitchen was tidy, they took their coffees into the living-room. Avoiding the sofa, Leah plopped down into an armchair, one leg tucked beneath her. She didn't think she would have any more problems with Hogan's waywardness but preferred not to take any chances by sitting too close.

'Why don't you switch from tennis to another sport?' she asked, taking a sip of coffee. 'One that would not put so much wear and tear on your leg.'

He looked at her as though she was talking nonsense. 'What do you suggest—tiddlywinks?'

'Golf.'

Hogan gave a guffaw of derision. 'You must be joking! You think I could switch to golf, just like that?' He clicked his fingers. 'I can assure you, my love, things are not that easy.'

The radar screen of her mind blipped when he called her 'my love', but Leah tried not to care; old habits die hard.

'And do you imagine it will be "easy" to continue with tennis?' she retaliated.

'No, but I'm familiar with tennis. Golf would be a step into the unknown and, to be frank, the unknown terrifies me,' he glowered.

'You said you were good at golf.'

'Hell, I'm not *that* good! It's only a hobby.'

'Exactly!' Leah pressed a hand into the air to emphasise her argument. 'The game is only a hobby and yet you're good. If you diverted your dedication from tennis to golf, might you not discover you could be *very* good? You already have the mental aggression of a winner, you respond well to pressure. Good grief!' she exclaimed when he continued to frown. 'You've always told me that the right mental attitude is what counts in sport.'

Hogan took a mouthful of coffee. 'There's more to it than that.'

'You are single-minded. You have good balance, quick reflexes, tactical awareness and a cool head— right?'

'Which doesn't mean I could play professional golf.'

'And it doesn't mean you can't have a damn good try.' Leah pushed up the sleeves of her sweater in determination. 'What have you to lose? You're no fool, Hogan, and even if you're not prepared to admit it yet, from the little you've told me it seems tennis could be a doubtful option.'

'But I don't know for sure,' he said doggedly, and gave a long drawn-out sigh. 'Even if the worst comes to the worst, does switching to another sport make sense?'

Her green eyes widened. 'But you've always maintained you thrive on competition, that you need a challenge.'

'I admit I thought that way once, but now I'm not so sure. Only over the past few weeks have I realised that my thigh could stop my rise back to Grand Prix tennis, and so far I haven't had the time or the courage, I guess, to think very deeply.' He shrugged. 'I'm in a state of flux and talking it over now, with you, is the first time the problem has been brought out into the open.' Hogan rubbed the thick dark hair at the back of his head. 'I don't know what the hell I'm going to do. Talk about peaks and troughs! My God, I've been peaking and troughing until I'm punchdrunk. Some days I have a cold dead ache at the pit of my stomach which tells me that without tennis I'm nothing—zero, zilch, damn all. But at better times I remind myself that I've always had a notion of my life outside the sport, which is more than some of my fellow players did.'

'That's why you've done so well with the sponsors. They prefer a rounded personality and some of the top guys were deadly dull,' Leah pointed out.

'And yet you have always felt I give too much of myself to tennis,' he said sharply.

She looked back at him over the rim of her coffee cup. 'Are you asking me or telling me?'

'I'm telling, and you're wrong, Leah. As an outsider I don't think you ever truly assimilated just what is involved. Top class tennis isn't a nine to five job. Fighting your way up to the top is hell. I've played matches which lasted for six or seven hours. Imagine, seven hours out on the court with hundreds of people watching every move! Not many other sports demand such intense concentration, so much physical endurance for so long.' He gave her a bleak smile. 'At times I've wanted to fling down my racket and run away and hide.'

'I know it's a hard life. I was new to that kind of dedication and perhaps I was jealous over the extreme hold it seemed to have on you,' she admitted, giving a rueful grin. She skidded away from the past. The future, Hogan's future, was what they should discuss. 'You could always enrol for a university degree as a mature student,' she said brightly, but meaning every word.

'Or open a sweet shop?' he drawled.

'How about running a tennis clinic?'

'I could take off as a model,' he said, grinning cheekily. 'With a handbag.'

'You could,' she agreed. 'Be serious, there are masses of careers open to you, if you think positively. You don't need to banish tennis in total, just so long as you choose a lifestyle that won't damage your leg.'

'The future scares me rigid,' he admitted in all seriousness.

'Naturally, but sooner or later you will be forced to reach a decision.'

Hogan grimaced. 'Going along blindly pretending my leg problem doesn't exist isn't very bright, is it?' While

I'm in Hong Kong I'll think around the subject and try and come up with some kind of formula.' He folded his arms. 'I'd be grateful if we could chew over any ideas together. You're a clever girl, so surely between the two of us we can find something for me to do.' He raised comic eyebrows. 'Something legal!'

'I'll be pleased to help.'

He smiled. 'Thanks. I'll need to have everything cut and dried before I let Saul into the secret. If he suspects I'm considering a change he'll start planning some horrendous publicity scheme.'

'He'll have a great time whatever you decide to do,' Leah commented drily.

'Not if I cancel my contract with him,' Hogan pointed out. 'By using the get-out clause I'll lose financially, but it'll be worthwhile if I escape Saul's dastardly ways. I'd feel much happier if I can conduct my life with a degree of dignity and not under the blaze of the Spencer circus strobes.'

'You'll have to do some pretty neat footwork to outwit him,' she warned.

They were to remember her words later . . .

CHAPTER SEVEN

AFTER vowing she would make not the slightest attempt to help Hogan during his holiday, Leah promptly executed a swift aboutface. He had, she decided when she recalled his promotional work, been remarkably amenable. The impression he had made in Hong Kong had burnished his name and likewise that of Spencer Associates, and her personal standing in the Colony's public relations world had gained several gold stars, too. Now she was happy to arrange a car to take him out to the golf club, speak to a travel agent friend about a day trip into China, steer him towards the best duty-free shops, and explain where he could hire a boat to sail around some of the two hundred and thirty-six islands. On occasion Terri and her man from Wisconsin went along with him.

'Can't you take time off and come with us?' he asked, tipping his head to one side and giving a beguiling smile.

She resisted his charm. 'Sorry, I can't. Now that Chinese New Year is over, the pace is quickening again.'

But though the days passed with Leah busy at the office while Hogan hit the tourist trail or played golf, every evening was spent together talking, talking, talking.

In retrospect it seemed their *only* previous communication had existed on a physical level, but now the verbal floodgates had been opened. Hours were spent discussing Hogan's future. One of them would float an idea which they would consider together—sometimes they would argue, there was criticism, frequently a chance suggestion was developed and extended, on occasions a notion was heaped with praise. All of a sudden they were the best of friends, sharing a mental affinity Leah had never dreamed possible and which delighted her. She couldn't wait to rush back to him each evening to talk over the latest scheme.

Yet illogically Hogan's willingness to settle for a platonic friendship began to rub her up the wrong way. True he called her 'kitten' and 'my love', and her mind's radar blipped accordingly, but the endearments were automatic. He made no attempt to kiss her goodnight, but merely wiggled his fingers or patted her bottom in the offhand manner of an older brother. She decided she was being contrary. It was a typical case of 'after you get what you want, you don't want it', but what did she want? Leah dreaded the answer, so she was forced to live with the footling discontent which whispered somewhere at the back of her mind.

The prospect of his departure in a few days' time was bitter-sweet. Hogan now sounded positive about the future. He would run his destiny, not be run by it and the prospect of a life without tennis no longer loomed like an abyss before him. She was horribly aware that he was perfectly capable of striding off into a brave new world, without her. But the sooner he was gone, the sooner she could put her own life in order, and the first step towards achieving that would be to forget all about him . . .

Leah gazed out of her office window, idly tapping her fingers on the glass. This morning a gusty wind was hurling sheets of rain across the grey harbour, where waves jostled in white-capped frenzy. Hogan had opted for what *he* classified as a lazy day; a two-hour workout in the Dynasty's gymnasium, museum tour after lunch, and then Leah had arranged to meet up with him for a swim in the hotel pool early evening. His training programme had been modified to take any strain off his thigh muscle, but he continued to exercise enough to convince outsiders that everything was normal. Tennis commitments in Hawaii would have to be met, so Hogan was maintaining his fitness peak for the present.

She smiled to herself, thinking how, after their swim, they would return to her apartment and doubtless indulge in more talking as she prepared an evening meal. She knew Hogan was structuring a final plan, though he had not told her his decisions yet. When the intercom buzzed into the silence, Leah jumped.

'Miss Tan again,' Violet told her.

'Put her through,' she said wearily.

Jasmine had been on the line every other day since her dance debut, demanding to know whether or not another booking had been fixed. In the hope that Hogan's conversations with Mr Tan might nip her problem in the bud, and remembering that Y.C. must surely be working on similar lines in the background, Leah had stalled. The phone calls were, however, now becoming frantic, and though her father's doubts about the economics of Jasmine's career were growing they were not growing rapidly enough.

This morning, after a brief greeting, the Chinese girl came straight to the point. 'The Gardens of Twilight. Why don't you contact them, or should I call round for an audition myself?'

'The Gardens of——' Leah choked on the last word,

wondering if she had heard correctly. 'Jasmine, you can't be serious!'

'You bet. Perhaps it's not as classy as the hotels, but it would be a foot in the door.'

'A foot in the gutter!' The Gardens of Twilight was a popular girlie bar which featured a late night cabaret. Leah had never been, but she had heard stories. 'I'll try the hotels again,' she gabbled, snatching promises out of the air. 'Don't you do anything until you hear from me and no, repeat *no*, auditions on your own. If you want me to handle your career then I organise the action!'

There was a long pause.

'But the Gardens of Twilight attracts many tourists, big shots from the States,' Jasmine said at last. 'A talent scout might be in the audience one evening.' Leah snorted softly. 'I've arranged a series of dancing lessons,' the girl continued when there was no further comment. 'And I've enrolled for singing class, too. It pays to be versatile. You never know, maybe I shall star in a musical one day.'

'Maybe.' Leah tried not to sound too disbelieving. She plucked at the ribboned cuff of her coffee-coloured Chanel-style silk jacket. 'And who's paying for all this training?'

'My pop, though he doesn't know it yet.' Jasmine gave a stagey sigh. 'Please hurry and fix a booking.'

'These things take time,' she prevaricated. 'The hotels arrange their programmes months ahead. It could be spring before——' She heard a howl of anguish. 'I'll do my best, just be patient,' she added hurriedly.

Leah let out a breath of relief when the line was cleared. Tomorrow Hogan was due to play golf again with Mr Tan, if the weather improved, so perhaps he could lard Jasmine's career dreams with further expenses? Certainly paying for dancing and singing lessons would not thrill the tight-fisted millionaire, and if additional classes for deportment and exercise were voiced . . .

'New York for you,' Violet said, when the intercom buzzed again.

'Saul here, honey.' It had to be Saul. No one else had lungs capable of blasting you into shell shock. She held the phone at a wary distance. 'Good news and bad news for that tennis ace of ours,' he boomed. Leah made a non-commital murmur. She had spoken with her boss to report back on Hogan's progress in Hong Kong, but had kept the conversation strictly to here and now. 'The good news is that there's another delicious bubble of publicity about to burst into the gossip columns. He should be congratulated.' Saul gave a shout of raucous laughter. 'Hogan sure has a flair for grabbing everyone by the throat. His timing is marvellous! This'll keep his name on everyone's lips until he starts back into professional tennis in a couple of months' time.'

What had happened now? she wondered. Saul must be exaggerating as usual. Hogan had mentioned nothing in the sponsorship pipeline and she hoped her boss hadn't arranged a promotional deal behind his back. The fewer fresh commitments the better, until his plans were finalised.

'Would you like to speak with him direct?' she asked. 'He's over at the Dynasty Hotel, I'll give you the number.'

Some instinct for self-preservation demanded she try to distance herself from Hogan's affairs. Their evening discussions were closeknit and eager, but she was becoming increasingly aware that she acted only as a sounding board. He would reach his decisions on his own, and when he flew out of Hong Kong he would be flying out of her life, forever. By insisting that their relationship remain platonic she was now unhappily aware she had guaranteed there could be no future for them together . . .

'Nah, you can pass on the information.' Saul guffawed again. 'Gee, I just wish I could see his face when he hears.'

'Hears what?' she asked, snapping on to red alert, for there was a gleeful malice in her boss's tone which boded no good.

'The bad news. At least, I imagine Hogan'll think it's bad news.'

'And that is?'

'The reason for all the fuss.' Saul was prolonging the agony.

'Which is?' she demanded.

'He's being cited in a paternity suit.'

'Oh!' she gasped, and the bottom fell out of her world. She couldn't think straight. Clutching the receiver, Leah stared blindly ahead, her nerves jangling, her thoughts rushing hither and thither like a headless chicken.

'Some girl in Norway has given birth to his son. She's another blonde beauty, something like yourself,' said Saul, brutally tying up an association which made Leah cringe. 'She and Hogan must have had something heavy going. What a guy!' Her boss sounded both envious and tickled pink. 'There's nothing like a spot of scandal to——'

'If you give me the particulars I'll ask him to ring,' she managed to blurt out, but she could scarcely hold the pen firmly enough between her trembling fingers to scribble down the facts.

'Tell him to phone as soon as he can, I'm just about to despatch a press release.'

'Oughtn't you to consult him first? He might not want anything made public. The whole thing could be false. You know how girls sometimes latch on to famous men and build up a fantasy world around them.' Leah was bleeding inside. The only way to protect herself was to refuse to accept Saul's story, but as desperately as she struggled to build a barrier, the more cruelly he ripped it down.

'Nah! Remember Hogan and that libido of his,' Saul gurgled. 'A paternity suit could be the best thing that's ever happened to him. Everyone loves a bit of gossip. We must capitalise on this, honey.'

'*You* can, but once he leaves Hong Kong he's beyond my range,' she reminded him.

And the sooner Hogan left, the better. Leah was close to tears. The emotional blow she had received was too much and she managed only monosyllabic replies until Saul ended his call. She buried her head in her arms, blinking hard, but after a few moments of silent grief accepted that there could be only one way forward.

'Violet,' she said into the intercom. 'Please would you ring the Dynasty and page Mr Whitney. I need to speak with him, it's urgent. I think he'll be in the gym.' During the interminable wait she fiddled with her hair, totally wrecking the sleek style until she had no alternative but to comb it all free and start again. When Hogan's call came through she had a mouthful of pins. 'Saul phoned and left a message for you,' she said, wildly jabbing pins into her head. Her voice was cracking and she knew there was no way she could pass on the news over the telephone. 'I'll meet you at my apartment in half an hour,' she gasped, and dropped the receiver as though it was red hot.

Leah spent the entire journey home rehearsing what she had to say. She always rehearsed scenes in advance, and now found herself living through a dozen different versions of how Hogan would react. He would be stunned, amused, flippant, delighted. Each version struck her as worse than the last. By the time she reached her apartment and was plugging in the coffee percolator, purely out of habit, her hands were shaking and her mind was in total disarray. When the doorbell pealed it sounded like a warning knell and she hurtled through the living-room propelled by nervous energy alone.

'What on earth's the matter?' asked Hogan, frowning down at the porcelain-pale of her face, dominated by the large green eyes which were troubled and overbright. 'There's bad news from home? Something has happened to my family?'

'No. Yes. No.' She stumbled back to the sofa.

'Kitten, tell me what's wrong,' he said, sitting beside her and taking her hand.

Her gaze skittered from him. She didn't want to cry. She wanted to be poised and uncaring. 'You're being named in a paternity suit. A Norwegian girl has given birth to your——' She gulped. 'To your son.' She grabbed away her hand to snatch the pad from the low table before them. 'Here's her name and address, and the relevant details.' She ripped off the top sheet and thrust the paper under his nose. She found it impossible to keep the bitterness from her voice when she added, 'Win some, lose some. You've had plenty of winners, Hogan, but this time you appear to have slipped up.'

He read and re-read the paper with a puzzled frown.

'I don't know the girl, and the last time I was in Norway was over three years ago.'

'So what? She could have been a one-night stand in Paris, St Tropez, London.' Leah gave a little laugh to show how blasé she was. 'I daresay one long-haired blonde is much the same as another, ten a penny, in fact!'

'What the hell do you know about it?' he asked angrily, his grey eyes burning into her. 'Okay, since we split I haven't been celibate, but I most certainly haven't run amok raping and pillaging as you seem to think.' His lip twisted. 'It's ironical that you choose to believe every innuendo tossed out by someone as loudmouthed and unreliable as Saul! I'm not a raving sex maniac, Leah. I did manage to remain faithful to you for three months and would have remained faithful to you for the rest of my life if you'd given me half the chance.' Scornfully Hogan flipped the paper aside. 'Whatever you may believe, I do have principles. I have never had a liaison with a stranger and I have never risked fathering a child. Strange to say this——' He flung the words at her. 'This *glamour boy* happens to be old-fashioned enough to put love and marriage at the top of his list.'

'I believe you.' Leah could not stop her voice from quavering. 'I told Saul there could be some mistake.'

'Then I'm in safe hands, aren't I?' he said with searing sarcasm. He was livid, his face a dark mask of anger. He rose swiftly to his feet and strode towards the telephone. 'How do I get through to New York on this thing?' he demanded. Weakly she went through the motions for him, but started to back away when the number rang out. He caught hold of her arm, his fingers biting into her flesh. 'You stay and listen, and listen *hard*! You handle my interests while I'm in Hong Kong, so you'd better make damn sure you take note of the instructions I'm about to give,' he sneered. 'Any slip up and you, and that piranha you call a boss, might well find yourselves with a suit slapped on you, too—for libel and slander!'

Leah stared at him wide-eyed, but managed to find her voice at last. 'That's not fair!' she spluttered indignantly. 'Ever since your accident you've gone along with Saul's promotion of your ... your wide-ranging virility, so you can't suddenly act the part of the outraged virgin now. You can't have it both ways.'

'Oh my love, but I can.' Hogan gave the facsimile of a smile. 'I admit I've never complained about the playboy image, but that was a lighthearted thing. It didn't hurt anyone. The girls I dated were models and actresses who knew what was involved, and who enjoyed appearing in the gossip columns.'

'And won't this Norwegian blonde enjoy that too?' she demanded, trying to prise his fingers from her arm.

'Get me Saul Spencer!' he barked when New York came on the line. He muffled the mouthpiece against his shoulder. 'This girl is probably some misfit who lives in a makebelieve world. She needs help, trained help, not a bevy of journalists beating down her front door to chivvy out salacious lies. Somehow she must be made to tell the truth and then face up to it, and the best way is to keep the whole matter confidential.' He glared at her. 'Don't you agree?'

Before Leah could reply Saul's fortissimo welcome sounded and Hogan's fingers tightened as he steered her against him, telegraphing a look which warned her to listen in to what was said.

'There's to be a complete news blackout on this

idiotic paternity suit,' Hogan growled, cutting through
Saul's smalltalk. 'And that's an order! I know damn
well you can keep the matter under wraps, it might
seem like world headlines to you but basically it's
peanuts. There's enough smut marketed already so this
item won't be missed.'

Leah heard her boss leap into a gratuitous protest.

'The whole story is a complete lie!' Hogan snapped.
'Get that straight! I don't know the girl, I've never
heard of the girl, and I intend to prove that her tale is a
total fabrication. Because she doubtless has problems of
her own, and because I have no intention of living out
some squalid wrangle beneath the glare of the media
spotlight, not a word is to be published. My lawyers
will be put on to the alert and should the slightest whiff
of libel or slander surface then the source will be
dragged through the courts, and that means *you*!'

There was silence at the other end of the phone. Saul
was uncertain, at a loss for words, which was a new
aspect of him as far as Leah was concerned.

'A private investigator is to speak with the girl and
obtain a statement. If she continues to cite me, he's to
take details of where and when the child was allegedly
conceived. After that, if she sticks to her tale, bring in
the police, but on a confidential basis. I'll search back
through my papers and prepare a statement of where I
was at the appropriate time.' Hogan gave a sour laugh.
'I'll bet money the girl and I were thousands of miles
apart at the vital period.'

'Well now——' Saul had started to recover, but he
was ignored.

'Arrange to have the child's blood tested and I'll have
a sample taken here and despatched by special express
to New York. Act fast and the whole matter will be

cleared up before I'm due to leave for Hawaii. If it isn't, I don't.'

'Say that again?' requested Saul, in disbelief.

'I don't move from here until the matter has been defused either by the girl retracting her statement, or by the blood tests proving I'm innocent.'

'But this isn't a simple operation, it could take time. Hell, Hogan, you know Hawaii is a major showcase. Our people out there have matches and interviews arranged, and there's an important cocktail party on the cards.'

In two terse one-syllable words Saul was advised what he could do with his cocktail party. More silence from New York. Leah had never known her boss to be stuck for a reply and decided it made a welcome change. When he finally managed to string some words together he was backing off like a fawning servant retreating from the presence of a demonical ruler.

'You're dead right, we must have this matter settled. Your reputation is at stake here. Muck like this paternity suit shouldn't be allowed to be spread around. I knew from the start it had to be a joke.'

'Some joke!' interspersed Hogan acidly.

'All the investigations wil be kept secret, don't worry.'

'I'm not. It's you who'll be worrying if you get hauled into court. A hefty dose of legal exposure won't do your profits much good, and if I have to sue for damages, I shall sue high!'

'Now let's keep a sense of proportion here,' Saul stammered.

'Get off the phone and into action!'

'Will do.'

When the line went dead, Hogan released her and

strode away, rubbing his jaw and thinking furiously. After a moment he swung back. 'Right, I want to draft a statement. I'll check my diary later so we can leave gaps for the relevant dates and places but I have a pretty fair idea of what I want to say. Well, don't just stand there,' he ordered. 'Get busy.'

Rubbing the tender part of her arm where his fingers had gripped her, Leah frowned. Everything had happened too quickly for her to take stock, but one thing was clear, the remainder of the day would be taken up in total with his activities. She heard the percolator bubbling in the kitchen. 'There's hot coffee, so shall we have a cup?' She glanced down at her chic suit. 'And I'd like to change if I'm not going back to the office. *And* I must ring Violet and warn her I won't be in.'

He scowled darkly. 'Good God! my reputation is being dragged through the mud and you want to drink coffee.' He gave a grunt of exasperation. 'Okay, but make it snappy. I'll have a cup, black. When we've drafted a statement we'll visit your doctor and he can take the necessary blood sample. It's to be on a flight to New York this evening. Afterwards we'll go and have that swim we organised.'

'I reckon we'll deserve it,' she said, trying to make him smile but he refused.

Five hours later she had still not been successful in making him smile, though as time passed the heat of his anger died, only to be replaced by cold feigned indifference which was worse. He deeply resented her initial belief that the paternity suit had substance, Leah knew that from the bleak disdain of his eyes, the hard clipped tone he used toward her, but whenever she attempted to justify her feelings he refused to listen.

Drafting the statement took ages. Hogan was determined to be concise yet comprehensive, and he had her changing around sentences and substituting words until she was dizzy. Eventually they reached the surgery and discovered the doctor had been called out on an emergency. With grim patience Hogan decreed they would wait, and spent the entire time pacing back and forth across the waiting room floor in methodical strides which wound up her nerves until she felt like screaming. She relaxed a little when the doctor arrived, hoping they would now be on their way to the airport within minutes. It was not so. An hour passed before the sample, neatly packaged together with a long list of technical data, was ready. It was late afternoon by the time they reached the airport terminal and by now Leah was fretful and edgy.

Hogan was sizzling. His blood pressure rose even higher when he realised that despatching a small parcel to New York was not a simple matter. Unknowingly they had wandered into a maze.

'Next desk,' the stewardess said with a big smile after Leah had explained at length what service was required.

The stewardess at the next desk, who had an even bigger smile, declared that her airline's flight had already departed but why didn't they try elsewhere? Elsewhere apparently consisted of joining one straggling queue after another, only to confront officials with bland smiles and no joy to offer. Hogan's face grew black as thunder. Leah gave a sigh of relief when a consenting airline was located at last, hoping he would stop muttering mindless threats. He did, for five minutes, but now they were sent scuttling between the airline's own departments, each situated as far apart as was diagonally possible. Technicalities arose; did blood count as mail, cargo or fall under the category of animal matter? The latter raised doubts as to whether the States would accept delivery.

'Can't you ask the pilot to slip it into his hip pocket?' Hogan growled and was rewarded with a big, big smile.

When the matter was finally resolved there were forms to complete—pink forms, yellow forms, forms in duplicate, forms which had to be pasted on to the package, English and Chinese forms.

'Everyone from the F.B.I. to the President of the United States to the Governor of Hong Kong must know that a few drops of my blood are on the move,' Hogan grumbled.

Leah flung him a scurrilous glance. Let him moan and groan! He could go and take a running jump! She had had enough, she was exhausted. Picking a way through the red tape had been taxing, but to do it in the company of a disgruntled, foul-mouthed male was *too* much! And she suspected that every complaint he had angled at the system's shortcomings had really been angled at her.

'Maybe it would be wise to have phials of your blood stashed away in each of the Spencer Associates offices worldwide,' she said, giving him a smile like stretched elastic. 'And then you'll be prepared should this problem reoccur.'

For one dreadful moment she thought he was going to hit her, there and then on the porch of the airport terminal but instead the hand he had raised produced a taxi.

'The Dynasty Hotel,' he told the driver.

Leah made round eyes. 'We're not going swimming now?'

'I've lugged the gear all around that damned airport

for god knows how long, so we're having a swim. A
swim will calm you down,' he added, pushing her
before him into the cab.

'Calm *me* down!' she protested, but he ignored her.

When they were on their way Hogan gave her a
shrewd inspection. 'You're not worried about meeting
up with Glenn at the hotel, are you?'

'No,' she said drily, staring out of the window. 'I've
already spoken to him on the phone a couple of times
about business and he didn't burst into floods of tears.
We can't avoid coming into contact, even if we wanted
to. Besides, he made a point of telling me he'd seen Sue,
and I gather she's helping him to rest and recuperate.'

'So as far as you're concerned, another redskin has
bit the dust?'

Eyes blazing emerald fire, Leah swung to him. 'That's
a mean thing to say! I was fond of Glenn, I still am. I
never set out to deliberately hurt him.'

'You never do, my love, you never do.'

She noticed that the driver was taking an interest. 'To
think I was misguided enough to believe that you and I
could ever be friends!' she hissed, before swinging back
to stare out of the window.

A Chinese lady in a black swimsuit and goggles was
churning up and down the pool like a myopic otter
when they arrived. Leah flounced off to the changing
rooms, taking her time to undress and slip into her
stretch satin *maillot*. The swimsuit was in bronze,
halternecked and cut high on the thighs so that her legs
appeared to last forever. It fitted like sealskin. When
she was ready she stood for a minute before the mirror
scowling and wondering why she had allowed herself to
be coerced into a swim which she didn't want, at a time

which was uncivilised and particularly in the company of a man she by now distinctly disliked. Hogan and the Chinese lady were sitting together on the edge of the pool, legs in the water, chatting happily when Leah emerged. Pretending not to know him, she dived into the deep end and swam several lengths of splashy crawl before her breath ran out. Afterwards she held on to the bar and examined the tiles.

'Goodnight,' she heard the Chinese lady say at the shallow end of the pool.

'Goodnight,' called Hogan.

Silence. Leah wanted to look round to see what he was doing but she refused to appear interested in him. She was deciding she would do one more length, then go and get dressed when two firm hands encircled her waist.

'Still mad at me?' a deep baritone asked.

She gave no acknowledgement until the hands slid up and round to cup her breasts, then she wrenched herself out of his arms. 'Isn't it mutual?' she demanded, galloping hand over hand along the bar until she was a safe distance away.

'You'd hurt my feelings,' Hogan said, flicking the wet hair out of his eyes. He swam closer, his tanned shoulders moving easily through the water. He was wearing brief black trunks and looked the picture of virile manhood. 'It didn't do much for my ego to realise my morality rating with you is zero.'

'Saul gave me the news as a fact,' she protested, turning to face him. 'I didn't have time to think. I was upset.'

'Why?' He stretched out two long arms to clasp the bar on either side of her, and his legs opened outside hers. She was trapped in a living cage, and the muscled bars were Hogan. 'Why were you upset, kitten? I've never seen you so unhappy. What difference would a paternity suit have made to you? It's almost two years since we split up, aren't we supposed to be platonic friends now, and no more? Isn't that what you've been trying to prove so earnestly this past week?'

'I haven't been trying to prove anything.' Leah wondered if she could duck beneath his arm and escape. There was too much male strength all around her. 'I was upset because, because ...' The correct phrases refused to line up for despatch while he was so close.

'You were upset because you still love me,' he said calmly and bent his arms, the water swilling over the bronzed muscles as he pulled closer. Now only inches separated them.

'No!'

He moved again, straightening his legs downwards as his fists curled tight around the bar, jamming himself against her. She could feel him against her from shoulder to thigh. Drops of water clung like brilliants to his black lashes, separating and glossing them. There were droplets, too, in his moustache. If she opened her mouth and put out her tongue, she would be able to taste them, able to taste Hogan.

Hurriedly Leah started to speak. 'We function better on a platonic level. It's been fun to talk and share ideas, and I think we work well like that. The physical side— our love affair—was good, but this is ...'

'Better?'

'Yes. I like you as a friend and I hope you like me as a friend. You'll be leaving Hong Kong in a few days so, please, let's keep things as they are. It's what is best. It's what both of us want.' She knew she was talking rubbish and so did Hogan.

The water eddied around them as he pressed closer, gliding against her. 'Can you feel what you do to me? There's nothing platonic about that!' His hand drifted to cradle her breast, circling the pointy peak with his thumb. 'And there's nothing platonic about that, either!' Leah was breathless, drowning in the deep grey pools of his eyes. 'We've tried it both ways, kitten, and neither way is complete. Now we shall try the third and final way.'

Though she was immersed in water, Leah was burning. A familiar flame began to lick over her, blurring her thoughts, softening her resistance. His fingers deserted her breast to catch at her chin, tilting until she was forced to decipher and accept his need, and reveal her answering desire.

'Tonight we shall sleep together,' he murmured. 'And every night——'

'Until you leave Hong Kong?' she blurted out, wanting to hurt him but hurting herself instead. Searching for the answer to a question she had not yet thought about.

'Until I leave Hong Kong,' he agreed with a sigh.

CHAPTER EIGHT

LEAH dried herself, pushing arms and legs into her violet sweatshirt and slacks with the frantic haste of someone about to leave a burning building, but as she raised a foot to zip up her boots, she came to a dazed halt. Okay, she loved Hogan but did he love her? And if he did, how strong and steady was his love? Commonsense warned she could be treading a tightrope, and how far could her heart afford to fall this time without breaking in two? But emotional responses have little to do with reason. All she knew was that Hogan would be hers for a few precious days and she was determined to grab all the happiness she could while she had the chance. If there was nothing else in the future, at least she would have memories. Live for the moment and to hell with the consequences, she told herself, and as she dried her hair, brushing it back into a burnished golden banner, she discovered her lips curving into a smile.

'Hello, kitten,' Hogan murmured when she joined him, and the endearment blipped gaily in her head. Leah's smile grew wider.

Encompassing her, his hand slid to her waist, and the strength of his arm, his masculine touch, made her melt inside and she laid her head against his shoulder. Being with him seemed so natural. By his side was where she belonged.

'We'll have something to eat in the coffee shop,' he decided. She was too slow in lowering her eyes and he

grinned, glimpsing her disappointment. 'Be sensible,' he
chided softly. 'Let's not spoil our first time together by
rushing things. It's been a hard day and we're both
tired. It's hours since we ate. Let's give ourselves time to
recuperate and enjoy a leisurely meal. What's the point
in us going back to the apartment and you having to
start cooking? We must pace ourselves. There's no rush,
is there?'

'Yes,' she said, her lower lip emerging like that of a
sulky child, but her eyes were shining. The heavy
sensual mood was broken and she was easy now.
Hogan was right, it made sense to move calmly,
savouring the pleasure to come. 'And it's not our first
time,' she protested.

'It sure as hell feels like it. My knees are distinctly
wobbly, never mind my thigh!'

When they reached the airy coffee shop, with its
rattan furniture and greenly-spilling plants, they sat
holding hands across the table, smiling foolishly. Leah
was grateful to discover that most of the tables were
empty and there was no one who appeared to recognise
Hogan. Right now she had no wish to share him with
an ardent fan.

'What you like to eat?' a waitress demanded in a sing-
song voice. She stood over them, oriental eyes bored
and disapproving, with her pencil poised.

To her amazement Leah discovered a menu had been
provided and gazed at the printed words, struggling to
make a decision. She was thankful Hogan had the
presence of mind to order wine and ask the girl to
return later for their orders.

'I still need to know something,' he said, when they
were left alone. She sensed that his mood had edged
into seriousness, and let go of his hand. He sat back in

his chair and folded his arms. 'I once said that our last few weeks together had been tricky, but I'm not taking all the blame. Something died between us, Leah, and *you* made it die.'

Her eyes were round as millstones. 'You knew!'

He gave a snort of anger. 'Do you think I'm stupid? Inch by inch you were separating yourself from me. A one-way retreat,' he emphasised. 'It was you from me.'

She didn't know whether to laugh or cry. 'I'm so glad,' she gasped.

'Glad I knew something was wrong?' He shook his head in frowning confusion.

'Yes, don't you see I imagined you had never noticed and that hurt. You carried on as though everything was fine while I rollicked around full of pain. I wondered how you could possibly love me when you seemed insensitive to what was happening. It was sheer torture.'

Hogan raised a barricading hand. 'Hold it a minute! Do I understand you deliberately chose to put a wedge between us?'

'Not exactly. You see——' She bit into her lip. So many emotions collided inside her head that she could not sort them out. 'I didn't want to draw back but Saul suggested——'

'Saul!' He spat out the name.

'What would you like to order?' The bored waitress had returned and was now tapping her foot on the floor.

Hogan glared at her intrusion.

'Fillet steak, medium rare, with a side salad,' Leah decided hastily.

'Make that two,' he added, with scarcely concealed impatience.

'Which dressing?' The waitress languidly smoothed

down the blackbird sheen of her hair beneath a starched white cap. Hogan produced a steady nihilistic stare in her direction, but she was unmoved. 'We have Thousand Island, blue cheese, French——'

'You choose,' he said.

Hong Kong was rife with odd foreigners, but the moustachioed man before her was one of the oddest, that much was certain from the way the waitress's mouth fell open. '*Me* choose?'

'Yes, write down whatever the hell you want.'

She remembered to close her mouth.

'French,' said Leah, coming to the rescue. 'For two.'

Chinese characters were scribbled down and the girl left, subjecting Hogan to a series of suspicious backward glances.

He seemed about to erupt. 'Let's get this straight. At Saul's suggestion you put our relationship out to grass?'

Leah felt distinctly uncomfortable. 'He suggested I back off a little in order for you to concentrate on your tennis, so I . . . I did.' The words gave the impression she had obeyed willynilly.

'Without one word of explanation to me!'

'But that was part of what was wrong, Hogan. In some mad way although I shared your bed I didn't share your confidence. It worked both ways,' she added quickly to avoid another outburst for his grey eyes were blazing. 'I'm not blaming either of us. We just hadn't built up the emotional trust. I was too unsure of myself, of you, of *us*. I was desperate to keep everything calm, not to upset you with Wimbledon only an arm's stretch away. I didn't tell you of Saul's suggestion because I thought you would be furious.'

'I would have,' he barked. 'But so what?'

His anger ignited an answering flicker. 'So at the time

I kept quiet and edged away because I believed it was
for the best,' she said through gritted teeth.

He gave a hiss of exasperation. 'If only I'd followed
my gut instinct and tackled you the minute I suspected
something was wrong!'

'Why didn't you?'

He hesitated, pouring out the wine before replying. 'I
guess I must have been as unsure as you apparently
were. I doubted our relationship was strong enough at
that time to bear an ultimatum. To be honest, I
resented your career because it kept us apart, but
equally I was all too aware of the excessive demands my
tennis made. Somehow playing the male chauvinist and
suggesting you ease off your career, while I went ahead
with mine, seemed very one-sided, though I confess I
was tempted to do just that! However, I persuaded
myself we were just passing through a sticky patch
which would end. Naturally Saul stirred up the issue by
telling me how dedicated you were to public relations.'

'Saul again!' Leah groaned, taking a mouthful of
white wine.

'Do you remember a meeting I had with him at the
London office just a few weeks before my crash?'

'Oh yes, I most definitely do! Go on,' she prodded
when Hogan looked curious, and after a moment he
resumed his explanation.

'Saul talked for hours about how important your
career was to you, stressing what a bright young lady
you were and that I mustn't be selfish and disrupt your
progress. It was the usual Saul overkill—blah, blah,
blah. The trouble is some of his arguments made sense,
and while he rolled on and on my mind was working
overtime. I reached the conclusion you didn't want a
deeper relationship because your work mattered more

than me.' Hogan took a slug of wine. 'I became all worked up inside. If I had had an ulcer, the damn thing would have burst!'

'I overheard some of that conversation,' she admitted.

He narrowed his eyes suspiciously. 'How?'

'I had come up to wait and Saul's office door was open, you opened it. You'd reached the part where you spelled out very clearly that what mattered most was tennis. You disowned me,' she said, making a weak attempt at a smile.

Hogan pushed the dark hair from his brow as he tried to think back. 'Oh God! Didn't I tell him I had no intention of getting married and pretended to accept his advice on having a few affairs on the side?'

Leah swallowed hard. 'You did, only it wasn't pretence. You did have affairs on the side.'

'Only after you had *gone*! When Saul mooted the idea, I went along purely to get him off my back. Half of my mind was on Wimbledon, I needed that over before I could reach any serious decisions about my future, *our* future.' He kept silent as the waitress slid platters of fillet steak before them and hurried away. 'You can't blame me for seeking reassurance when you left me in the lurch. Besides, I half hoped that if you read about the other women you'd get jealous and come charging back.' He lifted a brow. 'But you didn't. It was logical,' he protested when she just looked at him. 'I was hurt, you'd hurt me, and the girls bolstered my machismo.'

The on-off affairs were no longer important, and Leah couldn't keep the corner of her mouth from curving into a smile. 'Is that what you call it?'

When Hogan realised she understood, he smiled too. 'Why didn't you come back when you heard about the car accident?' he asked between mouthfuls of steak. 'Love doesn't end point-blank, kitten.'

'Actually I booked a flight the minute the news came through, but when I contacted Saul to advise him that I was coming to London he hinted that you and the Brazilian girl were . . . involved, so——'

Hogan slammed down his knife and fork. 'He should be hung, drawn and quartered! The way I read it, that bastard has effectively loused up eighteen months of our lives.'

'He did bring us together in the first place,' Leah pointed out, spearing a wedge of tomato.

'No, he's not having the credit for that. Okay, so you happened to work for him, but it was my decision that you looked after me.'

Her fork stopped in mid-air. '*Your* decision, how come? Surely my original assignment with you was part of a set training programme?'

'True, but another girl had been allocated. However, I'd seen you once at the office and liked what I saw, so I arranged to have you switched around. She ended up with a female opera singer, and you got me!' He was triumphant, the satisfied male.

'And you have the audacity to say *Saul* moves people around like pawns!'

To calm her down Hogan kissed his finger and dabbed it on to the end of her nose. 'So you see, as well as being a repressed chauvinist, I'm also a predatory animal,' he drawled with a contented smile.

'And a fixer!' Leah rebuked, but the warmth in her tone turned the description into a compliment.

'I couldn't allow Saul to have things all his own way.'

'Thank goodness.' She took a sip of wine. 'But why

did he send you out to Hong Kong? Was your visit legitimate or did he have some ulterior motive?' Hogan started to chuckle, a chuckle that grew into a laugh. 'Not you again!' she exclaimed in mock disgust. 'Between the two of you there doesn't appear to be much left to chance in my life.'

He brought his amusement under control. 'Kitten, I'd spent almost two years wondering what had happened to you and me. Again and again I tried to recapture the same feeling, the same *joy* but I failed miserably. I looked for you in every girl I dated. I'd reached the stage where I went into a trance if I saw a blonde on television or in the street who had even a vague resemblance to you. I became obsessed with wondering what you were doing, whether you had a new man, if you remembered me and still cared.'

The waitress stomped up. 'Want pudding?' she asked, whipping away their empty plates.

She stood by as Hogan inspected the glossy dessert menu, working his way down bright drawings of ice-cream sundaes and tropical concoctions.

'How about Sweetheart's Kiss?' he asked, winking at Leah as the girl shifted grumpily from one foot to another. 'A mouth-watering confection of limpid raspberries, the flesh of plump mangoes, a dash of cointreau and cool satisfying vanilla ice-cream?' She shook her head. 'No dessert, just two coffees,' he told the waitress briskly, and she gave a huff as she stuffed the unused notepad into her pocket. 'I bet she's gone back to the kitchen to grumble about two idiotic "foreign devils" who are too much in love to think straight,' he chuckled as the girl disappeared through a distant swing door.

'Are we in love? Are *you* in love?' Leah asked

carefully, not daring to look at him. Instead she gave devout attention to the last inch of wine in her glass.

'Yes.'

'Like last time?' The answer mattered very much and she held her breath. Last time he had loved her, but not enough.

Hogan strummed his fingers over the back of her hand. 'No,' he said thoughtfully, and she began to breathe again. 'Everything happened too quickly before. It was all delirious comings and goings. In those days I had a short-term focus and never planned further ahead than the next championship. I was very much in love with you, but I imagined you would always be there. I took too much for granted. I didn't realise anything worthwhile has to be worked for.' There was a wry twitch of his moustache. 'Our relationship shot off so rapidly that we never had a chance to get down to basics. I elbowed aside some of the time I had devoted to my tennis and squeezed you into the vacant slot, arrogantly assuming that was all it took.' He squeezed her fingertips. 'But this time around I'm older and, I hope, wiser. This time I have no intention of letting you go.'

'What would you have done if you'd arrived in Hong Kong and discovered I *did* have someone new?'

'God knows! I was desperate to see you. I decided I needed to exorcise you from my system, but the minute I saw you again I knew there wasn't a cat in hell's chance of *that* happening! One look into those gorgeous green eyes and I realised nothing had changed.'

Leah cupped her chin in her hand and looked at him. 'At one stage Saul reported that you didn't want to come,' she challenged.

He pulled down his mouth. 'I'd been having

problems with my leg and landed myself in a trough of
misery. Right then I couldn't visualise any future for
myself, let alone for us, and to be honest that was what
I secretly hoped for. Any ideas of sweeping you off your
feet when I was having difficulty standing on mine
seemed pathetic. What the hell did I have to offer as a
reject tennis player? Nothing!'

'I've never loved you because you played tennis. I
love you because you're you,' she pointed out.

'Yes, I know. But at the time I was plagued with
doubts, with insecurities. However, I'd plugged the
financial benefits of visiting Hong Kong so successfully
that Saul refused to let me slip off the hook, he virtually
forced me to come here.' Hogan gave a hoot of laughter
at the irony, and his infectious delight started Leah
laughing too. When the waitress came to hand over the
bill, they were both still enjoying the joke.

'Seriously,' Hogan said, taking a final gulp of wine
and trying to look serious. 'The sooner I rip up my
contract with Spencer Associates, the better. Once that
damn paternity suit has been cleared up Saul won't see
my heels for the dust.'

'Fine. I'll feel much happier if he isn't playing
Svengali in the background!'

He reached across to catch hold of her hand. 'You do
realise there might be repercussions? Saul will read
between the lines and discover I reached my decision to
quit in Hong Kong. He'll see you had to be involved. I
know it's your career, kitten, and I realise Saul's
company is a prestige company who pay well, et cetera,
et cetera, but——'

'But you'd like it if I leave him too?' she asked,
reading his mind.

Hogan gave a marvellous smile. 'I'm bending over

backwards here trying not to be the male chauvinist but yes, please!' He grinned. 'Now I can share my master plan with you. All week I've been wondering how I dare admit that you're included but you've been so damn prickly. You never truly imagined the sexual chemistry which exists between us could be ignored, did you?'

'Don't knock the last week, it worked!' she protested, chuckling at his growl of disbelief. 'If matters hadn't been kept platonic we would never have come up with all those wonderful ideas.'

'But now that we've finished being platonic am I allowed to come up with something wonderful of my very own?' he teased. 'Hurry up and finish your wine so we can get out of here and I'll show you exactly what I mean.'

They left the coffee shop beneath the baleful examination of the Chinese waitress. It was clear she regarded Hogan as an unknown quantity and even the tip he gave her was treated to a wary inspection, as though she didn't know whether she should expect gold sovereigns or plastic counters.

'So what's this master plan of yours?' Leah enquired as they strolled out to find a taxi.

'First we get married,' he announced.

'Aren't you supposed to ask, or is it a foregone conclusion?'

He stopped her in her tracks, placing both hands on her shoulders. 'Kitten, you and me winding up together was a foregone conclusion eighteen months ago.'

Leah had her secret doubts, but his masculine self-assurance was complete and he grinned back, determined to have things his own way.

'It'll be a relief to resign from Spencer Associates,'

she confessed. 'Saul's modus operandi has made me unhappy for a long time.'

'Wait until you've had a dose of my modus operandi,' Hogan purred with a Groucho Marx leer.

The leer may have been comic, but the look in his eyes was not. Ignoring the build-up of sexual tension between them was impossible and when he kissed her in the shadows of the taxi, a warm tremor swept over her. He held her close, touching her beneath her clothes, making her head spin with husky promises of what he would do to her, with her, for her . . .

'Stop it,' she protested, though there was nothing she wanted more than for him to kiss her and fondle her. But an inscrutable black gaze periodically peeked through the rear-view mirror and she was doubtful of the taxi driver's opinion of the two Westerners who were kissing and cuddling so ardently in the back seat. All the world might love a lover, but on this occasion Leah had her doubts.

'I'll behave,' Hogan assured her, sitting back to straighten his tie and rake his fingers back through his hair in an attempt at tidiness, but his eyes weren't behaving.

'Does your master plan decree whether or not my public relations career continues?' she asked, determined to be businesslike.

Hogan had other priorities. He selected a glossy strand of pale hair from her shoulder and began twisting it slowly around his finger. 'That depends.'

'On what?'

Coiling more and more hair, he bent closer until she could feel his breath warm on her face.

'On your private relations—me and the four kids.'

'Four!'

'They're in the master plan.'

'Hadn't you better reveal all the details, just in case I want to suggest some modifications?' Leah smiled. He was kissing her again.

'Tomorrow.'

She was beyond caring. 'Tomorrow,' she agreed.

When the taxi driver left them at the apartments he allowed the merest flicker of a smile to cross his face. Now Leah felt happy, comforted to know that behind the inscrutable oriental mask was a human being who understood what love was about.

The minute the apartment door closed behind them, Hogan hauled her silently into his arms. The effect of his lips against hers was as though a match had been tossed on to a petrol-soaked bonfire—*whoosh!* They were ablaze—petting, kissing, touching, snuggling, rubbing. Leah was lost in a delirium of desire and when, at last, Hogan raised his dark head, his mouth was swollen. She knew hers must be too.

'Bed,' he said throatily. 'We must go to bed.'

Scattering clothes right and left, they managed to reach the bedroom and then, somehow, they were clinging naked together between the sheets. Her blood raced as Hogan kissed her and stroked her. Every touch was magic. He was so strong, so deeply sure, his lips hard and demanding on hers as though he suffered an unquenchable thirst which only her mouth could satisfy. When he had drunk his fill, his kisses moved down across her neck and shoulders, teasing her silken flesh with the stiff bristles on his upper lip.

'Leah!' He breathed her name like a prayer. All the anguish of the time apart and all the pleasure of claiming her afresh throbbed in the word. 'Leah!'

With long fingers he caressed her, following the

curves, the dips, the hollows, the clefts which he
remembered so well, for how many nights had he held
her in his dreams? He cupped her breasts, murmuring
his pleasure, and as he traced his fingertips across the
sensitive peaks she sighed into his neck, straining
upward frantically. He eased down, murmuring her
name over and over. Leah was on fire, her hips sliding
against his, wanting the maleness of him inside her,
filling her deep inside, completing her. His mouth
slathered from one swollen pinnacle to the other,
nibbling and kissing, sending her skywards as she
pressed into him. A sigh shuddered through her as
Hogan touched her with lips and tongue as though
discovering her for the first time. The caress was
sensual, but then he demanded a response and she
moved against him, needing to possess and be
possessed.

'Leah!' Hogan moaned, sliding into her. They
paused, gasping against each other. The feel of him
was so good, and Leah knew a wave was building, a
huge white-crested wave which would break without
mercy, drowning them in love. 'Open your eyes,
kitten,' he commanded. How could she when she was
lost in the feel, the smell, the muscle of Hogan? But
somehow she dragged herself back from the edge of
ecstasy. His muscular arms and chest rose above her
like a gleaming bronze shield. 'I love you,' he said
with fierce intensity. 'I've never loved anyone but you.
'I'll always love you.'

'And I love you.'

He groaned, and it was the roar of the wave which
they could fight no longer. Leah pulled him down, her
nails marking the smooth flesh of his shoulders as
Hogan carried her with him, gasping and wimpering

into the crashing tumble of fulfilment. It was everything she ever wished, ever hoped for, ever needed to feel.

'Give the office a miss today,' he implored next morning. They had awoken in the night to make love and again when pale morning light showed behind the curtains. Now they lay cocooned together in warm, lazy bliss.

'Darling, I can't and, besides, you're due to play golf with Mr Tan.'

Hogan buried his face in her hair. 'I can cancel that. I want to make love to you again.'

'Right now?' she teased. 'Are you sure only your leg had reinforcements?'

'Well, maybe not right now,' he amended with a chuckle. 'Later, but not too much later!'

She placed her hand across his lips to quell his persuasion. 'I really have to go into the office, and you'll enjoy the golf.'

He opened his mouth and licked the top of her fingers. 'I'd rather enjoy you.'

'Come into the office this afternoon after your game and we can discuss your master plan.' Her eyes danced mischievously. If we leave matters until I get home this evening there's a possibility we could be sidetracked.'

'Okay.' He stretched slowly, muscled arms like bronze ramrods, then relaxed with a purring sigh.

Leah slid from between the sheets. 'Come on, let me see just how bad that leg of yours really is.'

'After a night of debauchery?' he asked, grinning at her. He sat on the edge of the bed, rubbing his thigh and then eased himself upright. 'Not too bad this morning.' Hogan pulled down his mouth in surprise as he tested his full weight on the limb. 'Still feels weak, but it's been a hell of a lot worse.'

'The break from constant tennis must be responsible,' she decided, heading for the bathroom.

Solemnly he shook his head. 'It's the sexual activity, kitten. I reckon more of the same three times a day for the next forty years and my leg'll just about recover.'

'The leg might, I wouldn't!' she retorted, scampering under the shower before he could put his remedy into practise.

Though Leah had expected time to drag until Hogan joined her, she was wrong. She went off to keep her appointment with the banker from the golf club and when he broke into their discussion to invite her to join him for lunch, she was surprised to discover how rapidly the morning had passed. Over their meal she explained methods of promotion, suggesting she draft a trial booklet listing the bank's spread of facilities, and also offering ideas for a dignified advertising campaign.

'You have given me plenty to think about,' the banker smiled as they parted. 'Thank you for all your help.'

She shone him a big smile. Whatever insults Saul might throw when he discovered that both she and Hogan were deserting his company, he could never accuse her of any failings as far as her work for him was concerned.

'Miss Tan's been on the phone, *three* times,' Violet droned when Leah returned to the office.

'Oh dear! Will you get her on the line. I'd better speak to her.' There was only one solution. She must ask Jasmine to take herself and her so-called talents elsewhere, whatever the consequences. Today Hogan would have done his best to paint Mr Tan a costly picture, but she doubted the matter would have been clinched. Jasmine's obsession with showbusiness could drag on for months, if not for ever! Her father was wrapped around her little finger, and Chinese family ties were strong. 'Good afternoon,' Leah said briskly, when the call was connected.

'I've rung three times already,' Jasmine pointed out, though she was not complaining, indeed she sounded buoyant. 'I have some wonderful news.'

Leah's heart sank. It seemed that the girl had taken independent steps and wheedled her way into some dubious cabaret.

'I don't think you're cut out for the entertainment world,' she announced, diving in head first. Her green eyes took on a determined glint as she attempted to combine diplomacy with brutal honesty. 'It's a cut-throat business and only the very best reach the top.'

'That doesn't worry me,' came the careless reply.

She took a deep breath and was involved in a lurid account of the trials and tribulations of showbusiness when Hogan walked into the room. She sign-languaged a greeting. For a moment he was content to wait, but as soon as he realised who was on the other end of the phone he leant forward and mouthed something. Shaking her head in distraction, Leah kept up her tirade.

'Hold it,' Hogan said loudly.

Momentarily she lost the thread of what she was saying and Jasmine leapt in.

'I agree with all you say. I'm ringing to ask you to cancel any booking and to remove my name from your list. I don't want any part of showbusiness.'

Leah echoed the last words, raising two eyebrows in astonishment. Hogan grinned in return and spread his hands in a 'there you are' gesture.

'Y.C. and I are to be married,' Jasmine explained. 'My career from now on will consist of learning to be a good wife.' She sounded as though she was hugging her happiness to her.

Leah managed to offer the right words of congratulations, listening wide-eyed as the girl bubbled on. When she replaced the receiver, she sat for a moment grinning at Hogan.

'Good old Y.C.!' she exclaimed.

'I was trying to tell you they're engaged,' Hogan said, coming round the desk to smile at her. 'Mr Tan was full of the news this morning. He reckons Y.C. is quite a catch and is hoping he'll join the family business.'

'It would be beneficial if he did. Y.C. went to Harvard Business School so he's full of bright ideas.'

'One of which is marrying a millionaire's daughter!'

'Thank goodness. He told me to use delaying tactics, but he's delayed Jasmine's showbusiness career for life.' She wiped imaginary sweat from her brow. 'He's saved me a hassle.'

Hogan pulled her to her feet. 'Us men do have some uses. Here's something else we're useful for.' He bent his head and kissed her, coaxing her lips apart.

'And what use is that?' Leah asked eventually.

'Makes you relax and feel soft and dreamy inside.' He cocked his head to one side. 'Am I right?'

'You're right.'

'You'd better have a further dose,' he murmured and his mouth was moving over hers when the intercom buzzed. 'Damn!'

Laughing, Leah freed herself and reached to flick the switch.

'Mr Spencer on the line,' Violet monotoned.

They shared a look of surprise as Leah picked up the phone.

'Any idea where I can reach Hogan?' bawled Saul, full-lunged as usual.

'He's here now,' she said, as muscled arms slid around her. 'It's for you,' she continued unnecessarily for every loud word was echoing through the room.

Hogan took the receiver, one arm still wrapped around her. 'Yes?'

'Great news about the paternity case. I had our London office fly an investigator out to Norway yesterday afternoon to speak to the girl in question. He's just rung through with the details and it appears she's retracted every single word. She has never set foot out of Norway, and she's never even seen you in the flesh.' He managed to lower his voice an octave. 'I guess she must have had a brainstorm.'

Hogan was stern-faced. 'Is there a child?'

'Yes, but no husband. I gather she's a promiscuous piece, the father could have been one of a cast of hundreds.'

'But not me! I want a signed affidavit as soon as possible, and go ahead with the blood test. We can't afford to leave any loopholes just in case the girl has another brainstorm at a later date.'

'Will do, will do. So now you'll soon be on your way to Hawaii,' Saul boomed happily.

'Yes, but advertise the matches as my swansong.'

'Pardon me?'

'Swansong, as in end of the road. I'm giving you notice here and now that my contract ends as from a month today.'

'You can't do that!'

'Yes I can, read the small print,' Hogan said coolly.

'There's a get-out clause.' He cut through the blabbering his words had incited. 'I'll be contacting my lawyers, they'll sort matters with the sponsors.'

'But why end a good run?' Saul wailed, beginning to realise the star money-earner for his company was in earnest.

'Because I've realised that to chance permanent damage to my leg by returning to professional tennis is downright foolish, and——' His arm tightened around Leah. 'Because I'm going to be married, and my wife and I intend to lead private private lives.'

A bellow made Hogan wince visibly.

'That minx Terri has double-crossed me! I told her an affair was okay, but never marriage. You don't need to marry her, she'll settle for less.'

'She might, but I won't,' Hogan replied, winking at Leah as he decided to go along with Saul's mis-understanding.

'Let me talk to Leah,' her boss demanded. 'Maybe she can make you see sense.'

Exchanging a wry smile, she took back the telephone. 'Hogan doesn't have any intention of returning to top class tennis and it makes sense. The muscle in his thigh wouldn't take the continual pressure.'

'To hell with his leg, the tennis is expendable,' growled Saul. 'I'll put out a press release explaining the situation and we can drum up a hell of a lot of sympathy over his predicament. But Hogan's a personality now, he doesn't need his sport. It isn't vital. He's been popular on interviews and chat shows and I know that angle can be promoted. He can earn a healthy living just so long as he stays single and maintains that glamour boy image. Don't let him get married, no one will swoon over him if he has a wife and is seen to be mowing the lawn or rearing kids like every other guy.'

'I'll swoon over him,' she announced.

There was a pause as Saul pondered her reply, for there had been a grain of intent running through her words. 'Look, honey, I know you fancied him once, but if he's serious about Terri——'

'Who said anything about Terri?' Hogan said into the phone. 'I'm marrying Leah.'

'Leah! but I thought——'

'We know damn fine what you thought. You thought you had finished off our romance nearly two years ago, but you miscalculated.'

'Now look here,' Saul started, but got no further for Hogan began to tell him where he could go and what he could do to himself, in graphic detail.

'I would like to give a month's notice, too,' Leah said, taking over the conversation before the language singed the walls. 'I have some leave accrued from last year, so when Roger returns in a fortnight's time I shall cease working for Spencer Associates.'

'But Leah, honey, surely we can work something out,' he spluttered.

Hogan jabbed a finger and disconnected the call. 'Saul will recover, once he's over the shock of our defection. He always does.'

Leah asked Violet to rustle up some coffee and they discussed her boss's foibles, both agreeing with the conclusion that even as they talked he was doubtless switching his allegiance to another up-and-coming sportsman or pop singer.

'Tell me about your master plan,' she said when Violet had deposited two brimming cups of hot coffee and tripped out, glancing sideways at Hogan all the while as she weighed up his 'go-to-bed' eyes.

'In the short term, when you've finalised matters here you'll fly out to join me in Hawaii. Once that's over we'll travel to London, tell all our relations about the wedding and arrange a date as quickly as possible.'

'Don't you think it would be wise to ask the surgeon to re-examine your leg?'

He smiled at her anxiety. 'Okay, kitten, I'll do that, but I'm convinced that once the tennis schedule finishes the muscle will revert to normal.'

'But what about the matches you have to play in Hawaii?' she fretted.

'If I lose, I lose. I promise not to go overboard on the fitness regime. Doubtless by then Saul will have informed the media about the weak muscle, and I'll be wallowing in sympathy from the fans. Ugh! the prospect makes me cringe but I suppose there's little point in making a mystery out of my retirement from the game.'

'Knowing Saul, he'll exploit the pathos for all he's worth,' Leah agreed.

'Once I'm free of Spencer Associates we'll keep a low profile, kitten. How do you fancy living in the country, preferably near a golf course?'

She grinned. 'So you're going to have a crack at professional golf?'

'It's an option,' he admitted. 'I intend to try out at the game, but there's no rush. Several paths are open to me and I'm determined to explore them all before I reach a final decision.' He took a mouthful of coffee. 'But my first priority is to marry you! Initially I'll have enough to cope with, having a new wife, a best friend and a mistress all rolled up into one.' He came round to pull her into his arms. 'If we buy an old house, something with character, we could renovate and furnish it together. Would you like that?' She nodded eagerly. 'Good. I've often wanted to try my hand at painting and carpentry.'

'Sounds like fun,' she agreed. 'But none of your fans will be thrilled to see you wielding a paint brush in place of a tennis racket. You do realise this will mean an end to your glamour boy façade?'

'Thank goodness! When Saul is off my back I intend to speak privately with a couple of my sponsors. Over the years some investment ideas have been raised, and now I have the time to devote attention to them. The owner of a group of international hotels once asked if I'd run summer tennis clinics, so perhaps we could consider that. Once I have the all-clear on my leg,' he added as a proviso when she looked thoughtful. 'I'd prefer not to abandon tennis completely at this stage. The sport has given me one hell of a life and I'd like to put something back in.'

Leah kissed his cheek. 'I quite agree.'

'And if you think of any other avenues I can explore, we'll talk them over.'

Now she kissed his moustache. 'Is that all we're going to do—talk?'

Hogan grinned. 'Fifty per cent talk, fifty per cent—love!' He bent to kiss her, holding her close against him. 'Forty-sixty,' he adjusted, his kiss deepening. 'Ten per cent talk and ninety per cent love,' he decided eventually and began to kiss her again. The office door opened. There was a giggle and an embarrassed apology before it quickly shut. Seconds later there were whispers in the outer office. 'That, I have reason to believe, is your reputation going up in smoke,' he murmured.

'You could be right. Violet is doubtless ringing round Hong Kong to inform everyone that I was caught kissing Hogan Whitney with the "go-to-bed" eyes.'

'I thought the phrase was "come-to-bed",' he said and jokily batted his thick dark lashes. 'Which is it, do you think?'

'Both.'

'And are they effective?'

Leah grinned happily. 'Every time.'

He took her hand and steered her towards the door. 'Then we'd better go. We can't disappoint Violet, can we?'

'Indeed not.'

A startled Violet watched as Hogan hurried Leah through the outer office.

'Miss Morrison will be back tomorrow morning, but late,' he said, over his shoulder and gave a broad wink.

She giggled and when she heard the hum of the lift, Violet dialled a number. 'Hey Pauline, what you think?' she began. 'You remember I told you about the man with the stay-in-bed eyes? Well, he and my boss are coming down in the lift right now and——'

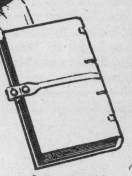

Enter a uniquely exciting new world with

Harlequin American Romance ™·

Harlequin American Romances are the first romances to explore today's love relationships. These compelling novels reach into the hearts and minds of women across America... probing the most intimate moments of romance, love and desire.

You'll follow romantic heroines and irresistible men as they boldly face confusing choices. Career first, love later? Love without marriage? Long-distance relationships? All the experiences that make love real are captured in the tender, loving pages of **Harlequin American Romances.**

What makes American women so different when it comes to love? Find out with **Harlequin American Romance!**

Send for your introductory FREE book now!

Get this book FREE!

Take these
4 best-selling novels
FREE

Yes! Four sophisticated, contemporary love stories by four world-famous authors of romance FREE, as your introduction to the Harlequin Presents subscription plan. Thrill to **Anne Mather**'s passionate story BORN OUT OF LOVE, set in the Caribbean.... Travel to darkest Africa in **Violet Winspear**'s TIME OF THE TEMPTRESS....Let **Charlotte Lamb** take you to the fascinating world of London's Fleet Street in MAN'S WORLD ....Discover beautiful Greece in **Sally Wentworth**'s moving romance SAY HELLO TO YESTERDAY.

The very finest in romance fiction

Join the millions of avid Harlequin readers all over the world who delight in the magic of a really exciting novel. EIGHT great NEW titles published EACH MONTH! Each month you will get to know exciting, interesting, true-to-life people .... You'll be swept to distant lands you've dreamed of visiting .... Intrigue, adventure, romance, and the destiny of many lives will thrill you through each Harlequin Presents novel.

Get all the latest books before they're sold out!
As a Harlequin subscriber you actually receive your personal copies of the latest Presents novels immediately after they come off the press, so you're sure of getting all 8 each month.

Cancel your subscription whenever you wish!
You don't have to buy any minimum number of books. Whenever you decide to stop your subscription just let us know and we'll cancel all further shipments.